Chapter 1:
Kake

CW01499761

1

When Sakyo Kataoka stepped off the train at Karasuma station in central Kyoto, he found himself underground – and with a decision to make.

Should he go up to ground level and walk, or change onto the subway? After much deliberation, Sakyo opted for the former. A professional dancer, he carried himself gracefully, skipping every other step as he ascended the long flight of stairs.

Leaving the station via exit number five, he found himself at the junction between Karasuma-dori and Bukkoji-dori. Judging from the dark blanket of cloud above, it was going to start snowing any minute. Sakyo turned up the collar of his coat.

'Excuse me,' he said to a businessman waiting to cross the road. 'Which way is Shomen-dori?'

'You mean down by Ohigashi-san?' The man's rough tone seemed somewhat at odds with his well-tailored suit.

'. . . *Ohigashi-san?* Is that the same as Higashi Honganji temple?'

'Course it is.'

'Then yes. That's where I'm trying to get to.'

'If I were you, I'd take the metro to Kyoto station, then the underground passage as far as Shichijo.'

'Right. The thing is, I actually just got off the train here, so I was thinking of walking . . .'

'That's quite a walk.' The businessman eyed Sakyo's delicate frame. 'Sure you'll manage?'

'I'm stronger than I look, I promise.' Sakyo threw himself into a lunge as if to demonstrate. 'I'll be fine on foot.'

'Guess it might warm you up at least. You want to head south down Karasuma. Cross Gojo, then it's left at the fourth set of traffic lights – just in front of Ohigashi-san.'

It seemed that in Kyoto even the businessmen spoke in dialect rather than standard Japanese. Maybe that wasn't so surprising, but Sakyo couldn't help feeling oddly impressed.

'Thank you!'

He walked south down Karasuma-dori as instructed, eventually reaching the wide avenue of Gojo-dori.

At the crossing, he rocked onto his tiptoes and hummed as he waited. An elderly couple gave him a bemused look.

Just before the signal turned green, an appetizing

THE MENU OF HAPPINESS

Hisashi Kashiwai was born in 1952 and was raised in Kyoto. He graduated from Osaka Dental University. After graduating, he returned to Kyoto and worked as a dentist. He has written extensively about his native city and has collaborated on TV programmes and magazines.

Jesse Kirkwood is a literary translator working from Japanese into English. The recipient of the 2020 Harvill Secker Young Translators' Prize, his translations include *The Kamogawa Food Detectives* by Hisashi Kashiwai, *Tokyo Express* by Seicho Matsumoto and *A Perfect Day to Be Alone* by Nanae Aoyama.

Also by Hisashi Kashiwai

The Kamogawa Food Detectives
The Restaurant of Lost Recipes

The Menu of Happiness

HISASHI KASHIWAI

Translated from the Japanese by Jesse Kirkwood

MANTLE

First published in the UK 2025 by Mantle
an imprint of Pan Macmillan
The Smithson, 6 Briset Street, London EC1M 5NR
EU representative: Macmillan Publishers Ireland Ltd, 1st Floor,
The Liffey Trust Centre, 117–126 Sheriff Street Upper,
Dublin 1 D01 YC43
Associated companies throughout the world

ISBN 978-1-0350-6071-9 HB
ISBN 978-1-0350-6073-3 PB

Copyright © Hisashi Kashiwai 2025
Translation copyright © Jesse Kirkwood 2025

The right of Hisashi Kashiwai to be identified as the
author of this work has been asserted in accordance
with the Copyright, Designs and Patents Act 1988.

Originally published in Japan as *Kamogawa Shokudo Itsumono* by Shogakukan in 2016.
Japanese/English translation rights arranged with Shogakukan through Emily
Books Agency Ltd. and Casanovas & Lynch Literary Agency S.L.

All rights reserved. No part of this publication may be reproduced,
stored in a retrieval system, or transmitted, in any form, or by any means
(including, without limitation, electronic, mechanical, photocopying, recording
or otherwise) without the prior written permission of the publisher.

Pan Macmillan does not have any control over, or any responsibility for,
any author or third-party websites (including, without limitation, URLs,
emails and QR codes) referred to in or on this book.

1 3 5 7 9 8 6 4 2

A CIP catalogue record for this book is available from the British Library.

Typeset in Galliard by Jouve (UK), Milton Keynes
Printed and bound in the UK using 100% Renewable Electricity by CPI Group (UK) Ltd

This book is sold subject to the condition that it shall not, by way of
trade or otherwise, be lent, hired out, or otherwise circulated without
the publisher's prior consent in any form of binding or cover other than
that in which it is published and without a similar condition including this
condition being imposed on the subsequent purchaser. The publisher does not
authorize the use or reproduction of any part of this book in any manner
for the purpose of training artificial intelligence technologies or systems.
The publisher expressly reserves this book from the Text and Data Mining
exception in accordance with Article 4(3) of the European Union
Digital Single Market Directive 2019/790.

Visit **www.panmacmillan.com** to read more about
all our books and to buy them.

CONTENTS

fragrance wafted over from a nearby hamburger restaurant. Sakyo swallowed the saliva that formed in his mouth and tried to ignore his growling stomach.

At the fourth set of traffic lights after Gojo-dori, he spotted Higashi Honganji temple on the right – or 'Ohigashi-san', as the businessman had called it. He turned left as instructed, and found himself on Shomen-dori.

Soon enough he was standing in front of a detached, two-storey building. With its nondescript, mortar facade, it didn't look like a restaurant at all. No noren curtain, no sign . . . and yet he could definitely *smell* something promising. It was all just as he'd been told.

He slid the door open a crack and, peering inside, called out: 'Hello?'

'Hi there,' replied a woman clad in a black sommelier's apron.

'Ah. Can I . . . come in?'

'Please,' replied the woman, pulling the door wide open.

'You must be . . . Koishi Kamogawa?'

'That's me.' She sounded a little startled.

'Right,' said Sakyo, removing his red puffer jacket. 'That makes sense. I was told to look out for the charming young detective, see.'

Koishi blushed. 'Flattery will get you everywhere.'

'I didn't make a reservation, I'm afraid. Any chance of something to eat?' Sakyo patted his grumbling stomach.

'Certainly,' came the voice of Nagare Kamogawa, emerging from the kitchen in his chef's whites. 'If you don't mind leaving the menu up to me, that is.'

'Sounds perfect.'

'Anything you don't eat?'

'Nothing at all.'

'Then just give me a moment.'

As Nagare returned to the kitchen, Sakyo sat down on one of the folding chairs at a table and began tapping away at his phone.

'So,' said Koishi, carefully wiping the table down, 'I assume you're not just here to fill your stomach.'

Sakyo looked up. 'Sorry?'

'You must have seen our advert in *Gourmet Monthly*. You know, *We Find Your Food*.'

'That's right. It was Akane, the editor, who told me where to find you. Look.' He tilted his phone screen in her direction.

Koishi glanced at the phone. 'Ooh, are you an actor or something?'

In the photo he had shown her, Sakyo was wearing a bright red full-length bodysuit and smiling alongside Akane.

'Not exactly.' He set his phone down on the table. 'I dance.'

'Ah. Is that mainly . . . avant-garde sort of stuff?'

'Well, *that* one was a little experimental, but I've done all

4

sorts. Period pieces, horror shows – I'll do anything, as long as I get to express myself physically.'

Nagare arrived with a silver tray full of food. 'Here we are.'

'Oh, wow . . .' said Sakyo. His whole body began to quiver as he eyed the various dishes being laid out in front of him.

Koishi put a concerned hand on his shoulder. 'Are you . . . okay?'

'It's just the anticipation,' replied Sakyo, his gaze riveted to the food in front of him. 'The sight of a spread like this. My body reacts when I get excited. Don't worry, it happens all the time.'

'Let me talk you through the menu,' said Nagare when he had finished arranging the plates on the table.

'Please,' said Sakyo, leaning forward.

'It's chilly these days, so I've included plenty of warm dishes. The fish on that small Awaji plate in the top left is yellowtail. Marinated in sake lees and then grilled – should be nice with a bit of the kuro-shichimi spice blend. Next to that, in the small Karatsu bowl, is chicken simmered with egg in a soy-and-dashi broth – basically the top part of an oyako-don, if you like. Tasty with a sprinkle of ground sansho pepper. To the right is the grilled turnip, to which you'll want to add a dollop of the fermented black bean miso. On the Shigaraki dish below that is roast duck wrapped in negi onion, which goes very well with this mustard paste. Next you have a palate cleanser: silken mozuku seaweed and mackerel, in a vinegar dressing. The Imari dish to the left of that is soy-braised softshell turtle. And the Oribe dish closest to you is spiny lobster simmered in white miso. I'll bring some rice out shortly.'

Sakyo, whose gaze had been flitting from dish to dish as Nagare explained their contents, let out a long, admiring sigh.

'It's even more stunning than I'd imagined. Akane did mention that you knew your way around the kitchen, but this is just . . .'

'Ah. So you know Akane.'

'We met through a collaborative project she was organizing. Dining and dancing, was the idea.' Sakyo was tapping out a rhythm with his fingers as he talked, though his eyes were still glued to the food. 'Must be three years we've known each other now. She invites me out to dinner parties every now and then.'

'Can I get you a drink?' Koishi asked.

'Do you serve wine, by any chance?'

'Nothing fancy,' explained Nagare. 'But I do have a few bottles of Japanese table wine.'

'A chilled white would be perfect.'

'Give me a minute.' Nagare slipped his tray under one arm and returned to the kitchen.

'You're a wine drinker, then?' asked Koishi.

'By process of elimination, more than anything. Sake and shochu aren't my thing, and neither is beer. So it's wine all the way.'

'Suits your image as a dancer, I'd say. Very refined.'

Nagare returned with a bottle of wine. 'How about this?'

'Wow,' said Sakyo, eyeing the label. 'I didn't even know Kyoto was a wine region.' He nodded decisively. 'I'd love to try it.'

'Toyosaka, it's called. From Amanohashidate. Made using Kyoto-grown Seibel 9110 grapes, with a dash of the German variety Bacchus.' Nagare removed the cork from the bottle and held it under Sakyo's nose. 'Nice citrusy aromas, don't you think?'

'You're right. That is lovely.'

'Drink as much as you like. Tastes best when it's only slightly chilled, which is why I've skipped the ice bucket.'

Nagare set a glass down at his side, then disappeared into the kitchen, followed by Koishi.

An abrupt silence descended. Sakyo quietly cleared his throat, then filled his glass. He found himself smiling at the contrast between the sight in front of him and the restaurant's somewhat bare interior.

He took a sip from the glass, nodded slowly in appreciation, then set it back down.

First he reached his chopsticks towards the spiny lobster.

It was on the small side, but had plenty of flesh on it. At the mention of white miso, he'd imagined a sort of heavy sweetness, but the aftertaste was light and refreshing, with a hint of yuzu. It was as though, instead of being left to stew in the miso, the lobster had simply been quickly basted in it. The flesh was translucent and, in the middle, only delicately cooked. This one dish was enough to convince Sakyo that he was in the presence of culinary genius. Even the refined ryotei restaurants his father had occasionally taken him to in Kyoto's Gion district seemed to pale in comparison.

When it came to yellowtail, he'd always thought a teriyaki-style glaze was the way to go, but the sake lees gave it a deep and complex flavour. Clearly, the chef hadn't just used the lees from some ordinary sake: the fish's flesh was infused with the aroma of a high-quality ginjo.

Moving on to the negi-wrapped roast duck, he added a little too much mustard, and found himself reaching for his wine glass to quell the fiery vapour that seemed to be coming from his nose.

When he was around halfway through the meal, Nagare reappeared.

'How are we getting on, then? Everything okay for you?'

'Oh, *more* than okay. I feel like dancing with joy.'

'Good to hear. The rice is ready, so let me know when you'd like me to bring it through.'

'Thanks. Think I'll enjoy this wine a little longer first.' Sakyo held his glass up in the air.

Next, he smeared the grilled turnip with the fermented black bean miso and began munching away at it. Another sip of wine, then on to the chicken simmered with egg. A liberal sprinkle of the sansho pepper and it was ready to be devoured. Sakyo poured more wine into his glass, the bottle's glugging growing higher and higher in pitch until there was hardly anything left.

He closed his eyes, recalling the performance he'd given three days ago. He'd thought it perfect, but the audience had been less convinced. It was a solo show, so he could hardly lay the blame at anyone else's door. He'd been so confident in the dance's structure and his own technical prowess that when the curtain had fallen unceremoniously on the stage without so much as a hint of a standing ovation, he'd felt crushed. In fact, crushed wasn't the word. It was like his very soul had been ripped out.

'Here's that rice,' said Nagare, setting two small earthenware pots down on the table. 'After all, we do need to talk about this dish you're looking for at some point . . .'

'Sorry! It's all just so delicious that I want to sit here all day savouring it.'

'Today's rice is cooked with crab. There's a bit of butter in there, too – sort of like a crab pilau.' Nagare removed the lid from one of the Shigaraki-ware pots and used a wooden paddle to spoon some of the rice into a small bowl, which he placed in front of Sakyo.

'That explains the slightly Western aroma,' said Sakyo, his nose twitching.

'Yes. That's why I thought I'd serve it with this, rather than miso soup,' replied Nagare, opening the lid on the other pot to reveal a chunky, Western-style soup.

'Is that . . . minestrone?'

'Something like it, yes. I've gone for the "double broth" approach that's all the rage in the ramen world these days. Made a kombu and dried-sardine dashi base, then added a bouillon I made from beef bones, together with some chopped vegetables and bacon. Anyway, I'll leave both these pots here too, so eat your fill.'

'I love minestrone!' said Sakyo, raising the bowl in his hands and taking a sip.

'When you're done here, I'll show you through to the office at the back. Oh, and here's some tea.' Nagare set a tall cup on the table, then withdrew once more.

Sakyo began alternating between large mouthfuls of the crab pilau and long sips of the soup, until the two bowls were empty. Then, after only a moment's hesitation, he refilled them both.

He'd been worried that, coming on the heels of the Japanese-style food he'd just enjoyed, a buttery pilau might taste a little too heavy, but his fears turned out to be groundless. This seemed to have something to do with the soup. It wasn't the flavour so much as the aroma, which had a sort of piquancy that cut through the pilau's intensity. The word 'spicy' wouldn't quite do it justice. It was something deeper than that – something almost *profound*, he thought, though maybe that was a dramatic way of putting it.

When he'd finished, he pressed his palms together in appreciation, took a sip from his teacup, and sat there deep in thought. He'd eaten his fair share of luxury cuisine in the past, French being a particular favourite, but he couldn't remember the last time a meal had satisfied him this fully.

'Right then, shall I show you through?' asked Nagare.

Sakyo rose halfway from his seat in order to bow. 'Thank you so much. That was . . . incredible.'

'I hope I'm not rushing you.'

'Not at all. I'm the one who was dawdling.'

Patting a light sweat from his forehead with a handkerchief, Sakyo got to his feet.

Nagare showed him to the end of the long, narrow corridor that led to the office of the detective agency, then knocked on the door.

'Come in!' called Koishi from inside.

'She'll take it from here,' explained Nagare, before returning to the restaurant. Sakyo walked into the office and sat down on a sofa, facing Koishi.

'Sorry to keep you waiting.'

'Dad's cooking is really something, isn't it?'

'I savoured every bite.'

'Sorry to jump right in,' said Koishi, setting a clipboard down on the table, 'but do you think you could quickly fill this out for me?'

'Certainly.' Sakyo began energetically scribbling away at the form.

'You even dance while you're writing,' grinned Koishi as Sakyo returned the clipboard.

'I think that's just how my body works by now. Sometimes I find myself jigging about while I'm brushing my teeth.'

'Sakyo Kataoka. That's your real name, then? I assumed it was a stage name.'

'Well, in a sense, it is.'

Koishi leaned forward. 'How do you mean?'

'As I wrote on the form, I come from a long line of Noh actors – the Kataoka family. My father, Seisetsu Kataoka, is the eighth generation. If I'd taken up his mantle, I would have assumed his first name, too.'

'A family of Noh actors. Huh. But . . . aren't you supposed to follow in his footsteps?'

'Well, exactly.' Sakyo smiled wryly. 'That's the problem.'

'But Noh is pretty similar to what you do, isn't it?'

'Oh no,' said Sakyo, almost cutting her short. 'Noh and contemporary dance couldn't be more different.'

Koishi flinched in surprise. 'How so?'

'Sure, they're both technically types of dance. But the movement is completely different. I mean, we don't even use the same verbs to describe it. *Odoru* can mean any old sort of dancing, but you only use *mau* for the restrained, sideways movements of Noh.'

'Right. Not quite sure I follow, but . . . why don't you start by telling me what dish you'd like us to find?'

'Kake soba.'

'Kake soba . . .' Koishi began scribbling in her notebook. 'That the same as su-soba?'

'If that's what you call it in Kyoto. Plain soba noodles in hot broth, without any trimmings.'

'That's the one. But . . . wouldn't that taste pretty similar wherever you ate it?'

'That's what I thought. Looking back now, though, I can't help feeling like there was something special about the flavour.'

'Where did you eat it?'

'Tokyo. A ryotei-style restaurant called Wakamiya, in Kagurazaka.'

Koishi's pen stopped moving. 'Wait. They serve *soba* in ryotei restaurants in Tokyo?'

'Not normally, I imagine. I think they served it up especially.'

'You're going to have to give me a few more details.' Koishi readied her pen once more.

'Like I was saying, instead of following in my father's footsteps, I've pursued a career in contemporary dance. Of course, he keeps trying to persuade me to come back to the fold. Turning up at rehearsals was one thing, but now he's begun visiting me backstage just before I'm about to perform, insisting we have a nice long chat about my future. I've already decided contemporary dance is my calling, and I have no intention of taking on my father's name and becoming a Noh actor. I keep telling him he's wasting his time, but he just won't listen.'

'This won't mean much coming from someone who doesn't know the first thing about dance, but . . . don't you think it would be best if you did carry on the family name? I mean, your poor father.'

'As selfish as it might sound, I don't want to devote my entire life just to keeping an old art form alive. If we're talking about the Noh that the great Zeami brought to perfection, then it doesn't really matter who performs it, as long as they follow his teachings. But contemporary dance is different. The entire performance comes from inside me. It's my own unique creation. Who knows? One day it might be considered a Japanese tradition in its own right.' Sakyo pursed his lips. 'I don't want to just keep Zeami's art alive, you see. I want to *be* the next Zeami.'

Koishi gave a deep sigh. 'This is all going a little over my head.'

'Normally, Father just says his piece and leaves, but once he invited me out for a meal instead. Must have been about three years ago. It was right after a performance. I'd spotted him sitting in one of the balcony seats, and after the curtain dropped he came to see me backstage.'

'And he took you to this ryotei,' said Koishi, scribbling away.

'I told him I'd prefer a bar or something – you know, somewhere a little more casual. A ryotei might be the sort of place a Noh actor would fit in, but a penniless contemporary dancer like me would stick out like a sore thumb.'

'Did your father think this was some sort of special occasion, then?'

'I guess so. But the wine we were served wasn't the sort of thing you'd expect at a ryotei, just some kind of table wine, and all the food was pretty simple – mainly dishes you normally order to nibble with a drink. What you'd call obanzai here in Kyoto. I was expecting Dad to broach some serious topic, but he just rambled away about this and that.'

'Fathers and sons aren't always the best at communicating, are they?'

Sakyo's gaze grew distant. 'In my case, he was always my

teacher, and I his disciple. I never got out of the habit of addressing him deferentially.'

'Doesn't sound like the easiest relationship.'

'Growing up, I thought it was normal.'

'And this is when you had the kake soba?'

'That's right. My father likes a drink, and between us we got through two bottles of wine. He doesn't normally talk about my performances, but that night he wouldn't stop criticizing me.'

'How do you mean? Not that an amateur like me would understand . . .'

'He kept saying this weird thing. That my dancing *drew too much attention to itself.* I mean, of course it does – I'm on stage!' Sakyo smiled bitterly, and Koishi followed suit.

'Noh actors really do live on a slightly different planet, don't they?'

'Eventually he seemed to realize he wasn't going to get through to me. He summoned the okami who ran the restaurant and murmured something in her ear. A few moments later, the kake soba appeared.'

'Not your average bowl of noodles, I imagine?'

'Well, that's the thing. See, I could hardly believe my eyes. I mean, there we were, sitting in a fancy Kagurazaka ryotei, and all we'd been eating was the sort of stuff you'd normally expect to see in a regular old izakaya. And to cap it all off, here was a bowl of ordinary-looking soba. I started thinking my old man might be playing some kind of prank on me.'

'But the noodles weren't so ordinary after all?'

'Actually, I didn't think much of them while I was eating them. The realization only crept up on me after we'd left the restaurant.'

'What did they taste like?'

'I can't really explain. There's nothing I can compare them to – all I can tell you is that it was a very subtle, sophisticated sort of flavour. One I'd never tasted before. The noodles themselves didn't have the soft feel of handmade soba, so they must have been the packaged type. It was the broth that was special. Not that I realized it at the time.'

'I have to ask: does this Wakamiya place still exist?'

'I'm afraid not.'

'Thought so. If it did, you could have just gone back there.'

'I had such an urge to try the soba again that I actually went to Kagurazaka in search of it,' said Sakyo a little sheepishly. 'But it seems to have closed for good.'

'Wouldn't your father be able to help?'

'I know it seems petty, but I don't want to depend on him like that.'

'I had a feeling you'd say that. Well, did this soba have any other distinctive features?'

'Have you ever had Tokyo-style kake soba?'

'Never,' replied Koishi simply.

'Well, the broth isn't the delicate type you have here in Kyoto. It's heavier on the soy sauce, which gives the noodles a slightly saltier flavour. Personally, I like it – but the kake soba I had at Wakamiya was something else entirely. The broth was almost completely transparent. The word that comes to mind is "refined". I've had Kyoto-style kake soba too, but it wasn't like that either. The flavour was really quite unique.'

'You're making me want to try it!'

'I've tried to find something similar at plenty of restaurants since, but it's never the same.'

'We could do with another hint. Something the taste reminded you of, for example?'

'You know, I like my food, and I've given this a lot of thought, but nothing seems to quite cover it. At a push I'd say it was a little like shio-ramen – you know, with the clear, salty broth? Warmed me up the same way, too.'

'Hmm . . . salty, eh? Dad's always saying the simplest flavours are the hardest to recreate.'

'That reminds me . . .' said Sakyo, staring into space.

Koishi leaned forward. 'Reminds you of what?'

'That soup your father served me just now. Something about it seemed similar to the soba broth, somehow . . .'

Sakyo broke into a smile. 'Sorry, what am I saying – minestrone and kake soba are nothing like each other, are they?'

Koishi made a note, then gave a sympathetic shrug. 'One last thing. What made you want to try the soba again, after all this time?'

'To be honest, I don't even know myself. I'd forgotten all about it – and then I got this sudden urge to eat it.'

'So it's not because you're thinking about taking up your father's mantle after all, then?'

'Not at all. Like I said, I know contemporary dance is my calling. It's just . . .'

'It's just what?'

'These days, I've finally begun to see why Noh is considered such an art form.' A twinkle came into Sakyo's eyes. 'I'd always thought of it and contemporary dance as two completely separate things, but I'm starting to see that they have quite a bit in common.'

Koishi grinned. 'See, what did I tell you? It's all dance in the end, isn't it?'

'Not exactly. There's still a world of difference between the two. I'm just saying there's a sort of . . . shared thread that connects them.'

'You're a man of firm opinions, I'll give you that,' said Koishi, her smile fading slightly.

'Come and see me perform sometime.'

'Sure,' said Koishi, snapping her notebook shut. 'Once we've tracked down this soba of yours.'

Sakyo gave a slight bow. 'Thank you.'

'Does sound a little tricky, I have to say.' Koishi got to her feet and tucked the notebook under one arm. 'But I'm sure Dad'll manage. He always does.'

Back in the restaurant, Nagare rose from his chair to greet them.

'Well? Did you get the whole story?'

'I did,' replied Koishi. 'This one's a real mystery, Dad.'

Sakyo bowed apologetically. 'Sorry if it's a tricky case.'

'Not at all,' grinned Nagare. 'Those are the ones worth solving.'

Koishi threw him a look. 'Easy for you to say that now, Dad.'

'Can I pay?' asked Sakyo, reaching for his wallet.

'That can wait until next time,' replied Nagare. 'When you pay for the detective service.'

'Right. And when will that be?'

'Cases usually takes us two weeks or so to solve. We'll be in touch.'

'Got it. I have a performance around then, so I might have to ask you to wait a day or two. Anyway, I'll be looking forward to it.' Sakyo bowed deeply, slid open the door – and was greeted by a tabby cat, who came trotting over to him. 'Oh. Is this your cat?'

'You could say that,' answered Koishi. 'But *someone*' – she glared at Nagare – 'has strong opinions about not letting animals inside.'

'It's a restaurant!' protested Nagare.

'Does it have a name?'

'We call him Drowsy,' replied Koishi.

'Well then, Drowsy.' Sakyo waved at the cat. 'I'll be back soon, okay?'

'Tough case, you said?' asked Nagare once they were back inside.

'Oh, the hardest yet, I'd say,' replied Koishi.

'What's he looking for?'

'Kake soba.'

'Ah. Tokyo speak for plain old soba in broth, if I'm not mistaken?'

'That's right.'

'Does sound tricky.'

'Right? And get this: it's from a ryotei in Kagurazaka that's gone out of business.'

'Oh dear,' said Nagare, his lips puckering like he'd just bitten into a lemon. 'What have we got ourselves into?'

2

This time, Sakyo arrived at the main Kyoto station – making it a lot easier to find his way to the Kamogawa Diner.

'Ah, Drowsy.' He crouched to stroke the cat sitting outside. 'Miss me?'

'I think he remembers you,' said Koishi, emerging from the restaurant and squatting at Sakyo's side.

'I've always had a soft spot for cats. But my father was pretty strict when it came to animals, too. Pets were a no-go.'

'Really? Did he think they'd affect his acting somehow?'

'Maybe it was the chanting he was worried about. Didn't want any stray hairs irritating his throat . . . or something.'

'Sounds like he ran a tight ship. Anyway, why don't you come on in?'

'Thanks.' Sakyo followed her inside.

'Welcome back,' smiled Nagare.

'Sorry if I've caused you a few headaches.'

'It did feel like a bit of a wild goose chase at first. But we got there in the end.'

'Well, I've been really looking forward to it.'

'Just give me a moment. I'll bring it through,' said Nagare, before retreating into the kitchen.

'You're quite the star,' said Koishi excitedly. 'I did my research after you left. New York, London – you've performed all over the place!'

'Thank you. That's what makes contemporary dance different from Noh: it's a universal language, one that transcends borders. I'd hate to feel like people were just watching me out of curiosity for some bygone tradition.'

'Now you've lost me again.' Koishi set a cup down on the table and, using a Banko-ware pot, filled it with green tea. 'Anyway, I just hope Dad has got this soba right.'

'I can't believe he managed it. I'd begun to think it might be hopeless.'

'He's never been one for giving up easily.'

Sakyo's expression stiffened. 'Sounds like my own father.'

'Here we go.' Nagare arrived with a blue-and-white porcelain bowl, billowing with steam, which he set down on the table. 'Not that it's much to look at.'

Sakyo leaned forward, then closed his eyes blissfully. 'What an aroma. That's just how it smelled, I'm sure of it.'

'Enjoy the meal – if I can call it that!'

'I'll savour every mouthful.' Sakyo pressed his hands together, then reached for his chopsticks.

'I just hope it's right.' With these words, Nagare

departed for the kitchen, indicating to Koishi that she should follow him.

When they'd gone, Sakyo simply sat there for a moment, chopsticks in hand, gazing at the soba in front of him.

Neatly coiled noodles, sitting in a bowl of perfectly clear broth: the dish in front of him was so simple it achieved a sort of purity. It was exactly how it had been at the ryotei. He tried to pick the bowl up, then quickly withdrew his fingers when he realized just how hot it was. He'd done that at the ryotei, too.

His heart pounding in his chest, Sakyo gathered the noodles with his chopsticks and tried a first mouthful.

'The same . . .' he murmured to himself.

He slipped a hand back under the bowl, tentatively this time, and, resting his thumb on its rim, tilted it towards him slightly and sipped the broth.

'Exactly the same . . .'

It wasn't just the flavour. The noodles *looked* identical – and so, he realized with bafflement, did the bowl itself. His memories were hazy, and he couldn't be entirely sure, but it did seem very similar to the one the noodles had been served in three years ago.

He inspected it more closely. Indigo-blue flowers on a white background. Peonies, probably, and wreathed with all sorts of leaves and vines. As his memories of the ryotei slowly returned, Sakyo sipped the broth and let out a quiet sigh.

A hush had fallen over the restaurant, broken only by the intermittent sound of Sakyo slurping on the soba.

Once he had finished the noodles, he cupped the bowl in both hands and slowly drained the broth into his mouth. Like a participant in the tea ceremony imbibing the last mouthful from his cup, he marked the meal's conclusion with a deliberate, quiet slurp.

He looked down and saw, visible now at the bottom of the bowl, the character for 'happiness'.

'There it is,' he murmured. Just as he remembered.

Right on cue, Nagare ducked through the curtain that separated the restaurant from the kitchen and came to stand at his side.

'How were they, then?'

'Incredible. And they tasted exactly the same.'

Nagare's face softened with relief. 'Ah, good.'

'I can't quite believe it. They were *identical*. How on earth did you . . .'

'Well, the quickest way would have been to ask your father.' Nagare grinned mischievously. 'But of course that wasn't allowed.'

'But Wakamiya isn't even in business any more. How did you get hold of this?' asked Sakyo, holding up the blue-and-white porcelain bowl.

'Ah. So I got that right, too,' replied Nagare, his grin widening.

'You did.' Sakyo dabbed the sweat from the nape of his neck with his handkerchief. 'I mean, if memory serves . . .'

Nagare sat down opposite him. 'I need to be honest with you about something. The truth is, the soba I served you today is entirely the product of my imagination.'

'Your . . . imagination?'

'See, ryotei like this are usually veiled in secrecy.' Nagare produced a faded photograph.

'That's the place.' Sakyo leaned forward and inspected the photo. 'Looks just the way I remember it, too.'

'Turns out the okami who was in charge of Wakamiya now runs a casual restaurant named Koraku, in nearby Suidobashi. I headed there straight away.' Nagare set a photo of this other establishment down alongside the first. 'Cosy little place. Ten seats arranged around a U-shaped counter – and when I walked in, almost all of them were taken. There she was, standing behind the counter, busily serving her customers their drinks.'

Sakyo picked up the photo of Koraku. 'It's tiny. Bit of a change from that fancy ryotei of hers . . .'

'I took a seat, ordered a drink, and asked her about the Wakamiya days. Now, I'm pretty sure she remembers you and your father well. But when I started quizzing her about the soba, she clammed right up. Probably my fault for asking so directly. She seems to have a rule about never discussing what went on behind the closed doors of her ryotei. It's the same with most restaurants like that here in Kyoto, so I knew better than to carry on prying.'

Sakyo nodded in silence.

'Just when I thought I'd hit a wall, the man sitting next to me revealed that he'd been a regular at Wakamiya. He'd never had the soba, but he was happy enough to tell me all about the other dishes he'd tried there.'

'Your persistence paid off, then,' remarked Koishi, who was also peering at the photo.

Sakyo tilted his head to one side. 'I still don't see how you . . .'

'It seems lots of the old Wakamiya regulars can be found at Koraku these days. Soon they were all telling me their own stories about the place. The okami didn't seem to mind – even put in a quiet word or two every now and then. Those stories led me to the soba you just ate. That, and a bit of deduction on my part.' Nagare glanced down at the empty bowl, a hint of pride lining his features.

'But it wasn't just the flavour. You even got the bowl right. I mean, with detective skills like this, maybe you should think about joining the police!'

Koishi glanced sideways at Nagare, but said nothing.

'Actually, in the end, it was the okami who gave me the biggest hint.' Nagare gave an embarrassed grin.

'Really?' asked Sakyo, cocking his head again. 'I thought you said she wasn't very forthcoming.'

'Well, one of the regulars mentioned something about how certain customers always asked for specific ingredients. Then the man next to me started chipping in with a few names.'

'And one of them was my father's?'

Nagare nodded. 'Then the okami said, in this low murmur: "There was that gentleman I always served our sea bream and softshell turtle soup. Which one was he again? I really can't remember . . ."'

'Sea bream and turtle?' commented Sakyo. 'Pretty extravagant combination.'

'That was when it hit me. She was trying to give me a hint.'

'Wait. Are you saying . . .'

'She went on: "Ah, that's right. Sometimes he even asked us to put somen noodles in it."' Nagare broke into a smile. 'Turns out the okami *can* be very helpful when she puts her mind to it.'

'So that's what was in the broth – sea bream and softshell turtle? Now that you mention it, it did taste like both those things. Even if my version came with soba noodles instead of somen.'

'I couldn't quite believe it myself at first. I assumed the rich umami of the turtle would drown out the delicate taste of the sea bream. But then I tried making it. Turns out the combination works a treat.'

'So it really wasn't your average soba that I ate, then . . .'

'That ryotei was a regular haunt for all sorts of celebrities and VIPs, so we can assume the okami spared no expense when it came to sourcing her ingredients. So neither did I: wild Akashi sea bream, and the same softshell turtle they use at some of the oldest Kyoto restaurants. If the sea bream was farm-raised, it might have been drowned out by the flavour of the turtle, but Akashi produce is something else. Absolutely packed with flavour. And yes, the noodles might not be fresh, but they're made using top-grade Hokkaido soba flour. They soak up the soup's flavours beautifully.'

Sakyo's expression had grown pensive. 'So that's what it comes down to. Using the genuine article.'

'Right. And when you use *two* ingredients like that in the same dish, they don't have to drown each other out. Sometimes, instead of competing for attention, they balance each other right out.'

'I tried simmering some rice in the broth, zosui-style,' said Koishi, 'and it tasted incredible. Those ingredients are a match made in heaven!' She paused and added with a shrug: 'Not that I'll get the chance to eat either of them again anytime soon.'

Sakyo was staring silently down at the bowl.

'It was the height of extravagance,' Nagare continued,

'but anyone who didn't know any better would think it was just a plain old bowl of soba. Your father kept quiet about what was in it – and the okami was careful not to give the game away, too. Which is why, at first, you thought you'd been served something a little simple. It's the same with the bowl. Using a dish made by the famous Rosanjin for some noodles is pretty indulgent, but if you didn't know better, you'd think it was just a regular noodle bowl.'

'Why didn't he tell me, I wonder? If I'd known, I'd probably have been a bit more grateful.'

'I can't tell you that. But there's that saying from Zeami, the old Noh master, isn't there? *What is concealed becomes beautiful.* Something tells me that might have something to do with all this.'

A faraway look came over Sakyo's face. 'Hmm . . . *What is concealed becomes beautiful . . .*'

'Again, this is just conjecture, and I might be wrong,' said Nagare, looking him right in the eyes, 'but I think that's the message your father was trying to get across.'

Sakyo returned his gaze. 'You mean he was trying to steer me back into the world of Noh?'

'I'm not your father, and I can't speak for him, but something tells me that's not it. No, I think he just wanted to share something that would help you *whatever* you ended up doing with your life.'

'The broth was made from sea bream and turtle, the

height of luxury, but it was presented to me as a plain old bowl of soba. And yet here I am, three years later, still unable to forget how it tasted. That's what my father wanted to show me?'

Nagare nodded slowly in response.

Koishi, meanwhile, was squinting in confusion. 'You've lost me again.'

'It's simple,' replied Nagare. 'To a parent, your child is always your child, no matter how old they get. You can't help but worry about them.'

'He does sound like a good dad.' Koishi turned to Sakyo. 'You *sure* you don't want to follow in his footsteps?'

'That's not what this is about,' replied Nagare on his behalf. 'What his father wants to pass on isn't a profession or an art form – it's a state of mind. Whatever path his son chooses, he wants to make sure he has the right attitude towards it. I don't think there's a parent out there who'd feel otherwise.' He got to his feet.

'Thank you so much,' said Sakyo, scrambling to his feet in order to give a deep bow.

'Still not sure I follow,' said Koishi with a confused grin, 'but I guess everything worked out in the end.'

'This has really helped.' Sakyo pursed his lips in determination. 'It feels like I can finally put all this behind me and get on with my life.'

Nagare bowed. 'Glad to hear it.'

'Now, let me pay. I owe you for last time, too.' Saikyo readied his wallet.

'We leave the fee up to the customer,' said Koishi, handing him a slip of paper. 'Just transfer however much you feel it was worth to this account.'

'Right. Well, those ingredients can't have been cheap. I'll make sure you're well compensated.'

'Let us know if you're ever performing in Kyoto. We'll be there, won't we, Dad?'

Nagare's face twitched slightly. 'Erm . . . yes. I guess we will.'

Sakyo chuckled. 'Don't feel obliged.'

'I can always bring a friend instead,' said Koishi, winking at him.

Sakyo bowed and made to leave. When he slid open the door, Drowsy sauntered over.

'Watch it, you,' said Nagare to the cat. 'You're not coming in here.'

'Not very nice to you, is he?' said Sakyo, crouching down to scratch Drowsy's neck.

'You can say that again,' said Koishi, squatting at his side.

'I keep telling you,' insisted Nagare, 'it's not a question of being *nice*. It's just—'

'Let me guess, Dad: you can't have a cat running around while people are trying to eat.'

'Right,' replied Nagare with a slight frown. 'Well, as long as you know the reason.'

'Mr Kamogawa,' said Sakyo, getting to his feet. 'Can I ask you something?'

'Go ahead.'

'It's about that soup you served me last time. The minestrone-style one. Something about it tasted similar to the soba I had at Wakamiya. Or is that just my imagination?'

'Well, this is a complete coincidence, but I think they must have shared an ingredient. Fresh ginger juice. Commonly served with softshell turtle – and presumably in that soba you ate. I only put a dash of it in the minestrone because I figured it'd help warm you up a little.'

'So that's why they tasted so similar!'

Nagare grinned at him. 'Quite the palate you've got there.'

'Thank you again for everything.' Sakyo bowed again, then set off down Shomen-dori – only to come to an abrupt halt. He turned and looked at them.

'One more question.'

'Of course,' replied Nagare, stepping forward.

'That character at the bottom of the bowl. The one for happiness. What do you think that was about?'

Nagare chuckled. 'Only Rosanjin could tell you that. Still, think about it. It's only once you've finished the bowl that you get to see it, right? I'd imagine it's the same when

you're up on that stage. What matters is how the specta-
tors feel after the curtain falls. If they can just depart from
their seats happy, I imagine that leaves the performer feeling
pretty wonderful too.'

Sakyo gave no reply. Instead, he simply gazed into the
distance, as if pondering Nagare's words.

'*Okibariyasu!*' called Koishi, wishing him well in the
Kyoto manner. This seemed to return Sakyo to his senses:
he swivelled on the spot and, head held high, set off once
more.

Halfway down the street, perhaps sensing that the two of
them were still watching him, he turned and bowed one last
time in their direction.

'*Dad!*' said Koishi, seizing him by the shoulders once they
were back inside.

'Easy there,' said Nagare, turning and breaking loose
from her grip. 'What is it?'

Koishi was glaring at him. 'I thought you said we were
cutting down on luxuries for a while. And then you go and
buy a *Rosanjin* bowl?'

'Oh dear, Koishi. Here I was, thinking you had an eye for
these things. It's a replica, obviously. With Rosanjin, they're
not hard to find.'

'Oh. Right. So . . . you tricked him?'

'Listen, he asked me to find his soba, and I found it.' Nagare lifted the bowl up to look at it. 'This was just a sort of bonus.'

'Can't blame me for thinking it was an original, though. I mean, you're always splashing out on things like that.'

'Actually,' replied Nagare, dropping his gaze, 'I'm not a huge fan of Rosanjin's dishes.'

'Why's that?'

'Nothing like hotpot on a cold night like this,' said Nagare, changing the subject. 'Sea bream and softshell turtle – not a combination you get to eat every day! Why don't you invite Hiroshi over?'

'Ooh, you think?' replied Koishi, her tone brightening. 'He does love a good hotpot . . .'

'As did Kikuko.' Nagare glanced at the family altar in the small tatami-matted living room that adjoined the kitchen.

Koishi went over to kneel by the altar. 'Probably would have told you not to waste money on such fancy ingredients. Isn't that right, Mum?'

'Oh, come on,' said Nagare, lighting a stick of incense. 'We're allowed a little treat every now and then, aren't we, Kikuko?'

Chapter 2:
Curry and Rice

1

When his train pulled in at Kyoto station, Nobuo Matsuba-yashi stepped down onto platform seven and glanced up at the nearby clock.

I could have been in Tokyo by now, he thought.

After leaving Kanazawa just before ten o'clock that morn-ing, the 'Thunderbird' had arrived at Kyoto at about ten past noon – a total journey of two hours and fifteen min-utes. Two weeks before, when he'd travelled from Kanazawa all the way to Tokyo, it had taken him just two and a half hours. The Thunderbird ran on regular railway lines: its speed was no match for the bullet train.

He was barely three steps up the stairs from the platform when he stumbled and only just managed to avoid falling over. Age seemed to be catching up with Nobuo fast.

He left the station by the Karasuma exit and followed the street of that name north. With nothing but a black satchel to weigh him down, he crossed Shichijo-dori at a trot before turning east down Shomen-dori.

When he'd arrived at his supposed destination, Nobuo lingered by the entrance, his head cocked sharply to one side. This wasn't what he'd imagined at all.

He stopped a young Buddhist priest who was passing by. 'Excuse me – do you know if this is Mr Kamogawa's restaurant?'

'I don't know about restaurant,' replied the priest in an unhurried tone, 'but yes, that's where you'll find him.'

'Right. Thank you.' Nobuo readied himself, then slid the door open.

'Hello?'

'Ah,' said Nagare Kamogawa, removing his white chef's hat with a smile. 'Glad you made it.'

Nobuo gave a quick bow, then stepped inside.

'Not quite what you were expecting?' said Nagare, glancing around the restaurant as if he'd read Nobuo's mind.

'Well, no. Bit of a surprise, I have to say.' Nobuo immediately regretted speaking his mind. None of the lacquerware he made was exactly on the cheap side, but the pieces Nagare had purchased for the restaurant over the years were among his most expensive. He'd imagined them in a slightly more upmarket setting.

'Hello there,' said a woman, bowing in his direction.

'Ah, you must be Koishi,' said Nobuo, turning to greet

her. 'Your father's told me all about you. What a charming young lady!'

Nagare gave a chuckle. 'Steady. It'll go to her head.'

Koishi, meanwhile, had turned red. 'Don't know about young – in fact, I'm not sure about "charming", either . . .'

But Nobuo wasn't the type to compliment people without good reason. And in this case, the reason was that Koishi bore an almost shocking resemblance to his own daughter, Yoko. It was less a matter of physical appearance and more that her expressions and gestures were identical.

'Now,' said Nagare, while Nobuo gazed at Koishi as if in a trance, 'is there anything you don't eat?'

'This'll sound odd coming from someone who grew up by the sea, but I'm not very good with raw fish. Especially sashimi . . . Otherwise, I'll eat anything.'

Again, Nobuo instantly regretted being so open about his preferences. He knew full well he was about to be served a Japanese-style meal, and here he was asking the chef to skip the sashimi – one of the cuisine's most integral elements. He knew this better than most people, because he'd spent the past half a century making the dishes it was served on.

But Nagare threw him a lifeline. 'I hope you don't mind me saying this, but did that come with age? See, it's the same with me. I'm never exactly thrilled when I stay at a seaside ryokan and they bring out one of those boat-shaped platters full of raw fish. Loved it when I was younger, though.'

'You too, eh?' replied Nobuo with a slight smile. 'Yes, I was fine with it when I was younger, but as the years go by I find it less and less appetizing.'

Koishi gestured towards one of the red-cushioned folding chairs at a table. 'Please – take a seat.'

'Food'll be ready in no time,' said Nagare, setting his hat back in place as he walked towards the kitchen.

'What'll you have to drink?' asked Koishi, positioning a large black lacquered tray that would serve as a place mat in front of Nobuo.

He peered up at her uncertainly. 'That depends on whether I'm allowed to treat myself.'

'I'd say you definitely are,' said Koishi. 'What have you got in mind?'

'Well, I actually brought this with me,' said Nobuo, producing a medium-sized bottle of sake from his satchel. 'It's good stuff. Thought I'd pair it with your father's cooking.'

'Gorin,' said Koishi, reading the name on the label. 'From Ishikawa?'

'Yes. Using local rice with Kanazawa yeast. I can't think of a better match for Mr Kamogawa's food.'

'You'll have to let him try some of it later. Shall I get you a tokkuri flask?'

'Oh no, I'll just pour it straight from the bottle. If you could fetch me a glass or a sake cup . . .'

'I'll bring some through for you to choose from,' said Koishi, and went into the kitchen.

Nobuo glanced at his surroundings once more.

We Find Your Food. Just as the single-line advert in *Gourmet Monthly* had promised, this was a real, old-fashioned shokudo, or casual restaurant. Back home, there were plenty of places just like it clustered around the station. Still, somehow, he'd never imagined that Mr Kamogawa of all people would run an establishment like this. Nobuo couldn't hide his disappointment at the cheapness of the interior: it was just so out of keeping with the lacquerware he'd sent here over the years. The tray Koishi had set down in front of him was one of his pieces – there was no doubt about that. And yet the table it was sitting on was surfaced with cheap laminate.

'Sorry to keep you waiting,' said Nagare, passing through the curtain that separated the restaurant from the kitchen. He had brought a selection of dishes, which he began arranging on the tray.

A rectangular Koimari-ware plate, an Edo Kiriko cut-glass dish, an Oribe-ware square bowl, and a small, painted Karatsu ware cup. Nobuo watched as, one by one, Nagare set them down wordlessly on the table.

'It's still hot in the daytime,' he said when he'd finished, as if by way of explanation. 'But the mornings and evenings are getting quite autumnal.'

Nobuo was so captivated by the food in front of him that it took him a moment to reply. 'Yes. What with the crickets chirping at night, it does feel like summer's almost over.'

'I'll talk you through it. The fish on the rectangular plate are autumn ayu, salted and grilled. One of them is lightly smoked over wood chips from a mixture of cherry blossom and apple trees; the other – with the roe – is marinated in a yuzu-infused sauce. Feel free to garnish them with the finely chopped water-pepper leaves on the side. In the cut-glass bowl is some late-season hamo eel, in a tangy nanban-style marinade. You could sprinkle some kuro-shichimi on there if you want to spice it up a little. Oh, and don't worry: all the fish is cooked right through! The Oribe bowl contains today's fried dishes: the breaded chunks of autumn aubergine and Omi beef are best paired with the miso sauce; while these two – surf clam and vegetable tempura, and fried kuruma prawn fishballs – will go nicely with the matcha salt. And the Karatsu cup is filled with a mixture of miniature taro, baby matsutake mushroom, red konnyaku jelly and okra. I'll bring your rice and soup through a little later, so for now, just nibble away and enjoy that sake.' Nagare tucked his long, rectangular tray under one arm and bowed.

Koishi arrived with a bamboo basket containing at least

twenty sake cups, which she set down next to the lacquered tray. 'Take your pick.'

Nobuo crossed his arms and grinned. 'I can hardly choose.'

'Well, I'll leave them here, and you can pick one out,' Koishi said, twinkling, before following Nagare back into the kitchen.

Nobuo selected a Shigaraki cup from the basket and filled it with the sake.

As he brought the slightly oversized cup to his mouth, Nobuo gazed down at the spread that now filled the lacquered tray in front of him.

Here he was, in the sort of casual eatery you'd expect to find in some out-of-the-way neighbourhood – and yet if he kept his eyes glued only to the tray, he could easily have been in some Michelin-starred ryotei. The selection of dishes, the way the food had been arranged on them, the food itself – it was all of the highest order. He must have sat there staring for a good two or three minutes before, finally, he reached for his chopsticks.

First he tried the ayu filled with roe. The refreshing citrus fragrance of the yuzu gave way to the rich flavours of the well-matured fish – with autumn around the corner, it would have been nearing the end of its life cycle when it was caught – and the satisfying 'pop' of the tiny eggs as they burst in his mouth. Nobuo was well into his sixties, and he'd eaten ayu countless times over the years, but it had never tasted this exquisite.

When it came to the nanban-style hamo eel, he did as instructed, sprinkling it with the kuro-shichimi – a blend of spices and crushed black sesame seeds. *Ah*, he thought, *Mr Kamogawa did say this was late-season hamo.* That explained why the eel was less fatty than usual – which, together with the tartness of the vinegar-based marinade and the heat from the kuro-shichimi, made for an aftertaste that was invigorating rather than overbearing.

The respective strengths and weaknesses of each ingredient had been balanced against each other perfectly in a display of sheer culinary skill. This was the work of a master cook – that much was certain. So why, he wondered, hadn't Mr Kamogawa fitted this place out with the decor to match?

But by the time he bit into the deep-fried Omi beef, he had begun to see things a little differently.

If you were served dishes like this at one of the high-end restaurants you found in Kyoto's Gion neighbourhood, you'd be more than happy with it – but the impact wouldn't quite be the same. It was the very ordinariness of these surroundings, Nobuo realized, that had heightened his surprise – and delight – at the food.

The bottle of sake was still half full, and yet he'd almost

finished the food. Just then, with perfect timing, Nagare arrived from the kitchen.

'How about that rice I promised?'

'That'd be wonderful. To be honest, I could happily sip away at my sake all day, but at some point I do need to talk to you about this dish I'm looking for.'

'The food was alright, then?'

'*Alright*? It was one marvel after another. You know, in my line of work, I find myself being treated to meals often, but I've never had anything quite like this.'

'Oh, I don't know about that,' said Nagare, smiling softly as he cleared away the dishes. 'This is a humble old place, really.'

'To be honest, it did come as a bit of shock at first. To think that my work was being used in a restaurant like this, I mean.'

'I'm sorry to disappoint.'

'Don't be. I see now that it's all a grand strategy on your part.' Nobuo grinned broadly at Nagare, who departed for the kitchen with a slight frown on his face.

'You look like you could do with some more sake,' offered Koishi.

'Oh no, I've had plenty.' Nobuo screwed the cap firmly back onto the bottle. 'In fact, I should probably sober up a little.'

'Today's rice is mixed with hamo eel,' said Nagare,

returning with a Shigaraki-ware clay pot and a small, lidded bowl.

'Interesting. I've had hamo as sushi plenty of times, but never with regular rice.'

'Well, it's certainly not as fancy as sushi,' replied Nagare, setting the pot down on a woven straw mat. 'Anyone could whip it up at home.'

'And what's the soup?' asked Nobuo, removing the lid from the small bowl.

'I chopped up the skin from the hamo and made it into dumplings. Add a bit of this yuzu peel too, if you like.'

Nagare appeared to have deliberately used one of Nobuo's creations to serve the soup. A tempting fragrance was rising from the jet-black lacquered bowl.

'Regular green tea alright for you?' asked Koishi, showing him a Kyo-ware teapot.

'Oh yes. In fact, at home I like to have a cup of bo-cha.'

'Bo-cha?' repeated Koishi, pausing with her teapot at the ready.

'A speciality of Kaga, back in Ishikawa. It's a sort of roasted green tea – like hojicha, basically, but made using the stems rather than the leaves. It's all about the fragrance.'

'Nothing like it after a good meal, is there?' Koishi poured the green tea into a tall, narrow cup, releasing a smoky aroma.

'This is just a small portion for now,' said Nagare, placing a bowl of rice in front of Nobuo. 'But there's plenty in the pot, so just tell me if you'd like more.'

Nobuo's eyes widened. 'This is the . . . hamo rice?'

'Almost looks like plain white rice, doesn't it? I broke up the flesh from some grilled hamo and mixed it into the freshly cooked rice, then added some finely chopped sansho pepper leaves and shredded perilla for seasoning. Really ties the flavours together. And if you're wanting to pour that tea over your rice and eat it chazuke-style, I'd recommend adding some of these toppings: wasabi, nori seaweed and crumbled rice crackers.' Nagare set the wooden spatula he'd used to serve the rice down on the lid of the clay pot.

'I didn't realize the hamo flesh would be this white without the skin,' said Nobuo, reaching for his chopsticks. 'It's practically gleaming!'

Just as Nagare had said, it looked like little more than regular white rice. But as he raised a clump of it towards his mouth, the potent smell of hamo reached his nose first. The rice was clearly packed with the eel's flesh. Meanwhile, its skin had been used to make the dumplings for the soup. Somehow, this determination not to let any ingredient go to waste seemed typical of Nagare's style.

By the time Nobuo had refilled his bowl twice, pouring tea over the third serving as Nagare had suggested, the clay pot was almost empty.

'Could do you a whole extra pot if you like,' grinned

Nagare, who had reappeared with his tray tucked under one arm.

'Oh, no,' said Nobuo, rubbing his stomach. 'I've had plenty already. In fact, I can't remember the last time I ate this much rice in one go. The best meals really are a labour of love, aren't they?'

'Glad it was to your liking. Now, once you've had a little time to digest, we can talk about this dish you're looking for. Just let me know when you're ready.' Nagare cleared the dishes from the table and retreated once more.

Even if he was still struggling to reconcile the simplicity of his surroundings with what he'd just been served, Nobuo was by now quite certain that the food itself was of a high enough standard to more than compensate for that discrepancy – and that with Nagare as his detective, he was in safe hands.

He took another long sip of his tea, then rose from his seat and called out that he was ready.

The restaurant was built in the traditional Kyoto machiya style: despite its narrow frontage, the building stretched a long way back from the street. Walking slowly and deliberately, Nobuo followed Nagare down the hallway that led to the office.

'What are all these?' he asked, stopping to look at the photos that covered almost the entirety of the walls on either side.

Nagare turned to face him. 'Dishes I've made over the years. These photos are how I keep track.'

'You . . . don't just make Japanese food, then?' asked Nobuo, leaning in to inspect one of the photos.

'Oh no. Chinese, Western – I'll try anything.'

'So you're good enough to cook high-end cuisine, but you still bother with second-grade dishes like ramen?'

'I don't mean to contradict you, but I've never really believed in "grades" when it comes to food. The idea that, for example, kaiseki cuisine is somehow "superior" to ramen – it just doesn't sit right with me. At the end of the day, I'd say all that matters is whether the person cooking the food and the person eating it each understand where the other is coming from.'

'If you say so . . .' murmured Nobuo, clearly unconvinced.

Lacquerware, too, came in all sorts of styles and grades – but the only kind Nobuo produced was the very finest. In the past, he'd crafted more ordinary dishes, for everyday use, but his acquaintances in the trade had belittled him so much for it that he'd ended up focusing on producing only the most refined ware. If the name Nobuo Matsubayashi carried any weight in the world of lacquerware these days, it was because of that decision. It was the same with cooking, he thought: there simply *was* such a thing as status. And when it came to ramen and kaiseki cuisine, the difference in status was just too great to ignore.

Nagare knocked on the door at the end of the corridor, and they were greeted by his daughter.

'Please, go on in. Koishi will take it from here.'

Nobuo felt a slight pang of disappointment. He'd assumed it was Nagare who was going to be doing the detective work. He watched the chef retreat down the corridor – then, feeling more than a little uncertain about all this, sat down opposite Koishi.

'If you could just fill this out, please,' she said, sliding a form across the table separating them. As requested, he wrote down his address, full name, age, date of birth, family details, occupation and contact information.

'Right then, what's this dish you'd like us to find?'

She was gazing at him steadily, her eyes gleaming with determination. It was exactly the way Yoko had always looked at him. For a moment, he found himself simply staring back at her.

'Hard for you to talk about, is it?' asked Koishi, breaking the silence.

When Nobuo replied, it was in a voice so faint as to be barely audible. 'Curry and rice.'

Koishi readied her pen. 'From a restaurant?'

'No.' Nobuo was still looking straight at her. 'My daughter made it for me.'

Koishi glanced at the form he had just filled out. 'That would be . . . Yoko?'

'That's right. Eight years ago.' He let out a short sigh, then looked up and let his eyes roam the ceiling.

'Then . . . can't you just ask her to make it for you again?'

'If it were that simple,' responded Nobuo in a deflated voice, 'I wouldn't be here, would I?'

'Of course. Sorry.' Koishi bowed her head.

'Two years ago, Yoko took someone's life. She's in prison now.' Nobuo sounded somehow detached from the words that had just emerged from his mouth.

There was a pause. Then, peering uncertainly at him, Koishi asked, 'Do you . . . think you could tell me a little more about that?'

'My wife died young. I raised Yoko, our only child, on my own – as best as I could. Saw her all the way through high school and into a Kyoto university.' His expression darkened as he went on. 'It was an all-women Christian university, where the students lived in a dormitory, so I figured I didn't have anything to worry about. But while she was in Kyoto, she fell into the clutches of a real deadbeat.' Nobuo gave a derisive smirk, though it seemed to be directed more at himself than anyone else.

'I guess fathers feel that way about pretty much any boy who tries it on with their daughter, don't they?'

'No, this was different. He really was a pathetic excuse for a man. Head stuck permanently in the clouds. All he did was write these fantasy novels – *speculative*, I think he called them. The sort of drivel that was never going to earn him a single yen.'

'That's not so bad, is it? Who knows – he might be famous one day.'

'Listen, I might not be a writer, but I make things for a living. I know talent when I see it – and this guy didn't have an ounce of it. Yoko realized that too, I think, which is why she decided she'd earn a living for both of them. That's the sort of caring person she is.'

'What's wrong with a woman being the breadwinner for a change?'

'Oh, it's easy to say that in the abstract. But imagine if you were her father – how would you feel then?' Nobuo spoke so forcefully he could have been addressing his own daughter.

'That . . . might be different, I guess . . .'

'I raised her to always look out for others. Turns out I probably shouldn't have. When I told her I didn't approve of him, she refused to listen. Said they were going to get married regardless.'

'And in the end, they did?'

Nobuo nodded wordlessly, then went on. 'After that, Yoko and I broke off all contact. I mean, she'd chosen a man like that over me. What else was there to say?'

'Is there some sort of connection between that marriage and this . . . incident you mentioned?'

'They'd been married six years at the time and had a son together. I got a phone call from the police, telling me my daughter had killed someone.'

Koishi's eyes widened. 'Not her . . . husband?'

'That might have been easier for me to accept.' Nobuo gave a faint smile. 'See, I don't really know much about these writer types, but it seems they like to get together and . . . discuss things. And sometimes those discussions get out of hand, and they end up hurling insults at each other – or worse. Anyway, Yoko and her husband were out drinking at an izakaya one evening when another writer really started laying into him. The pair got into a scuffle, and when Yoko stepped in and pulled them apart, the other writer ended up smacking his head on a nearby pillar.' He let out another short sigh. 'Turns out the blow landed in exactly the wrong place.'

'Oh no . . .' said Koishi, her voice welling with sympathy. 'What are the chances . . .'

'It was the victim who had started the whole thing, and everyone was quite drunk, so there were plenty of mitigating circumstances – but there was no getting around the fact that she was directly responsible for his death.'

'What happened to her husband?'

'When Yoko went to prison, he left their son behind and ran off to some island down south – Ishigaki, I think it was. Fed Yoko some nonsense about how he'd be able to focus on his writing there.' Nobuo furrowed his brows. 'Now, if he was a painter I might understand – following in the footsteps of Gauguin and so on – but this is a writer we're talking about. What good is living on an island going to do?'

'About this curry and rice. You said Yoko cooked it for you eight years ago. Which would be *before* she went to prison?'

'Yes,' sighed Nobuo, his gaze drifting back up to the ceiling. 'A week before her wedding.'

Koishi was struggling to find the words to reply.

'After university, they moved to Tokyo together. With me still so opposed to the match, she never came home. All I'd get was a phone call from time to time.'

'I'm sure she missed having you in her life.'

'When she did finally turn up that day, it was in a last attempt to win me round. I'd told her I wasn't coming to their wedding, you see. She asked if the two of us could at least have dinner together.'

'Okay, you weren't happy with the match,' said Koishi,

her tone hardening, 'but couldn't you have at least attended the ceremony? I mean, poor Yoko . . .'

'I wasn't going to stand there and ask a man like *that* to look after my daughter,' replied Nobuo, his nostrils flaring. 'Not in a million years.'

'But you wouldn't be saying it for his sake. You'd be saying it for Yoko's.'

'Well, she knew me too well to press the issue. Said she just wanted to make me her curry.'

'The poor thing . . .' murmured Koishi, her eyes glistening.

'I love curry, see. I must have eaten hundreds – no, thousands of plates of the stuff over the years. But none of them can match the one she made that day.'

'I'll bet. I mean, for all she knew, it could have been the last time she'd get to cook for her dear father . . . Go on, then – what sort of curry are we talking about?'

'Well, the most unusual thing about it was that the rice was all mixed into the curry. I almost did a double-take when she set it down on the table.'

'*Rice mixed into the curry*,' repeated Koishi as she noted this down. 'Anything else?'

'The flavour itself was quite mild, but in terms of heat it was definitely on the spicy side. By the time we'd finished, even Yoko had broken into a sweat.'

'Sauce aside, what were the main ingredients?'

'Tender-braised beef. There were none of the usual

potatoes or carrots, or any other vegetables. Oh, and there was some sort of mincemeat in there too.'

'Sort of like a keema curry, then? What sort of colour was it?'

'Quite a dark brown, which makes me think it had red wine or something in it.'

'Did Yoko say anything about it? For example, that she'd been trying to replicate the curry from a certain restaurant, or that someone had taught her the recipe?'

'All she talked about was the venue and plans for the wedding, and that idiotic fiancé of hers. She barely even mentioned the curry – and neither did I.'

'If you liked it so much, couldn't you at least have told her? That way, she might have let you in on a few more details.'

'It wasn't really the time or place. She was just so focused on getting me to change my mind.'

Koishi clicked her pen repeatedly in frustration. 'This is going to be tricky.'

'She was never much of a cook herself. My guess is that she based it on something she'd had in a restaurant.'

'That *would* make things a little easier . . .'

Nobuo leaned back against the sofa. 'I suppose it could have been something she ate in Kyoto.'

'Whereabouts in the city did she live?'

'The dormitory was right by the university. Over in Higashiyama Sanjo.'

'And she lived there the whole time she was a student?'

'That's right. Until she graduated.'

'Did you ever visit her?'

Nobuo shook his head and snorted slightly. 'Couldn't. Her dormitory was women only.'

'Then I'm guessing you don't know much about the sort of life she lived. You know, any part-time jobs she had, or clubs she was involved in.'

'She did seem to be making the most of her time as a student. I'd get these letters once in a while, with photos of her visiting the temples at Nara, or camping by Lake Biwa.'

Koishi crossed her arms. 'Not sure if that gets us any closer to the curry.'

'It's not like it was a favourite dish of hers growing up. But she did seem to like trying new restaurants. And Kyoto has plenty of temptations in that regard.'

'Still, it's hard to imagine your average student managing to recreate the exact curry she'd had in a restaurant.'

'I'd have to agree with you.'

'There's our mystery, then.' Koishi flicked through her notebook as if deep in thought.

'Maybe she ate it at the dormitory cafeteria,' muttered Nobuo all of a sudden.

'Could be a possibility. Now, tell me, what made you suddenly want to eat this curry again?'

'I want my grandson to try it,' said Nobuo, smiling for the first time since he'd entered the room.

'That'd be . . . Fuminori?' said Koishi, again eyeing the form he'd filled out earlier.

'Just turned seven. He's got such a good head on his shoulders that you'd never know he had such a joke of a father. Doesn't mope about his situation, either – probably out of consideration for his mother. And well behaved into the bargain.'

'Grandkids really are a joy, aren't they? People say you get even more attached to them than your own children.'

'We always wanted a boy, too. That might have something to do with it.'

'Does Fuminori live with you, then?'

'Yes. I took him in after what happened with Yoko, and I've looked after him ever since.'

'Isn't it tricky balancing your work with the childcare?'

'My younger sister helps with that side of things.'

'That's . . . Yoshie, right?'

'Yes. She never married. She's been looking after him like her own child.'

'Nothing like family to help you out of a bind. But . . . didn't you say this curry was on the spicy side?' Koishi tilted her head doubtfully. 'Can't imagine that going down very well with a seven-year-old . . .'

'I was worried about that too. But it turns out he loves spicy food,' said Nobuo, his features creased into a smile again. 'Must get it from me.'

'I can tell he's the apple of your eye.'

'Please – find the curry for him, if not for me.' Nobuo lowered his head into a bow.

'Leave it to us – or to Dad, I should probably say.' Koishi grinned as she closed her notebook.

Back in the restaurant, Nagare looked up from the pot he was washing, then turned off the tap.

'Manage to explain what it is you're after, then?'

'Oh, yes. Koishi did a very good job.'

'Dad, you've got your work cut out for you this time.'

'*This time?*' replied Nagare, smiling ironically as he wiped the pot dry. 'You mean, unlike all those other times when I had it easy?'

'Mr Kamogawa, thank you very much for agreeing to help,' said Nobuo, bowing in his direction.

Nagare bowed back. 'I'll give it everything I have.'

On his way out of the restaurant, Nobuo stopped and turned. 'Oh, and about those soup bowls you ordered. They should be done in a couple of weeks. I'll send them as soon as they're ready.'

'Actually, that's perfect timing. We ought to have tracked down this meal you're looking for by then, so why don't you just bring the bowls with you when you come back?'

'Right then. I'll do that.'

Just then, Drowsy appeared and began curling himself around Nobuo's legs.

'Enough of that, mister,' said Nagare, shooing the cat. 'You'll get fur on his clothes.'

'Is he yours?'

'As good as, yes,' explained Koishi with a pout as she scooped Drowsy up. 'But *someone* never lets him inside.'

'Can't have an animal running around while I'm serving people food.'

'Oh, it's the same for me,' said Nobuo with a grin. 'If a single hair were to get mixed in with the lacquer . . . My grandson wants a cat, though. And they really are adorable.'

'You could always have one that lives outside, like us.'

Nobuo chuckled at Nagare's suggestion, then turned and set off down Shomen-dori.

'It's curry, Dad,' said Koishi when he'd disappeared from view.

'Hmm. I had him pegged as the type to go for something a little fancier.'

'He could barely get the word out at first.'

'Is there something unusual about this curry, then?'

'Not really,' said Koishi, setting Drowsy back down on the ground. 'Just the fact that it's mixed up with the rice, apparently. I have a pretty good idea of the sort of thing he's after.'

'You do? Well, that speeds things up. How about you take this one?'

'Don't be ridiculous.' Koishi thumped her father on the back. 'What'd happen if I got it wrong?'

2

'Are we there yet?'

Fuminori was looking up at Nobuo with a disgruntled expression.

'Just a little further, I promise. Come on.' Nobuo tightened his hold on his grandson's hand.

When, after heading north up Karasuma-dori, they turned onto Shomen-dori, it was with a mixture of anticipation and anxiety that he adjusted his grip on the boy's hand.

They arrived in front of the Kamogawa Diner. 'When we walk in,' said Nobuo, straightening his posture, 'make sure you say hello nicely, okay?'

'Okay.' Fuminori twitched his nostrils. 'Ooh, I can smell curry!'

Nobuo slid the door open gently and stepped inside. 'Hello?'

'Ah, good to see you,' said Nagare, appearing in his chef's whites.

Fuminori came to attention on the spot, then declared, in a loud voice: 'Hello!'

'Hope you don't mind that I brought him along,' said Nobuo, looking uncertainly at Nagare.

'Oh, he's more than welcome.' Nagare bent down and ruffled Fuminori's hair. 'Thanks for coming, kid.'

'Here are those soup bowls, by the way.' Nobuo handed Nagare a gift bag.

'So you're Fuminori!' said Koishi, squatting at Nagare's side. 'You're okay with spicy curry, then?'

'Yeah,' said the boy with a slight pout. 'If it wasn't spicy, it wouldn't be curry.'

'Not *yeah*, mister,' said Nobuo, placing a firm hand on Fuminori's head. '*Yes.*'

'I made a separate portion, thinking you'd be taking it home to him. A bit less spicy than yours. I'll serve him that one, in any case.' Nagare straightened up again, then hurried off to the kitchen.

'Sorry.' Nobuo bowed to Koishi, who was busy arranging two place mats on one of the tables. 'I should have told you I was bringing him.'

'Not at all,' she said with a grin. 'We're lucky to meet him.'

'I can't believe he managed to find it in just two weeks,' said Nobuo, joining his grandson at the table.

'Well, this is Dad we're talking about. I don't think you'll be disappointed.' She turned to Fuminori. 'But *you'll* let us off if it's not quite right, won't you?'

'Yeah – I mean, *yes*!'

'You really are a good boy, aren't you – just like your grandfather said. But you can relax here, you know.' She massaged his shoulders slightly. 'There's no need to be so formal.'

'I thought it'd be good to get him used to spicy food in advance, so last Sunday I took him to a local curry place. He had the "medium spicy" and polished it off in no time!'

'Really? Sounds like you're already doing better than me.' Koishi leaned towards Fuminori's ear and whispered, 'I can usually only handle the "mild" option!', eliciting a grin.

'My wife was the same,' said Nobuo cheerfully. 'It wasn't just curry – she couldn't stand anything that packed a kick. But Yoko must have taken after me, because she loves a bit of spice. Even when we took her out for sushi as a kid, she'd always ask for extra wasabi. Looks like Fuminori here has inherited it, too.'

'Koishi, could you lay the table?' called Nagare through the curtain separating the restaurant from the kitchen.

Koishi set two spoons, their ends wrapped in paper napkins, down on the place mats, followed by two glasses of chilled water.

Fuminori stood up and tried to peer into the kitchen. 'I can't wait to try it.'

'Exciting, isn't it?' replied Nobuo, following his gaze.

'I sampled some,' said Koishi as she set out small plates of salad and pickles on the table. 'It's good, I can tell you that.'

'Alright, here we are,' said Nagare, arriving with a plate of curry which he placed in front of Fuminori.

Nobuo peered down at it from his grandson's side. 'Oh yes – that looks just right.'

Fuminori leaned in for a sniff. 'It smells . . . amazing!'

'Sorry to keep you waiting,' said Nagare, returning with a second plate and setting it down in front of Nobuo.

The curry was served on a thick-rimmed Tachikui-ware plate. The way it had been presented – flattened into a sort of round disc that covered most of the plate – was just like when Yoko had made it. So, too, was the silky lightness of the sauce, the way it seemed to have seeped into every grain of rice. There were the cubes of tender braised beef – five of them – sitting on top of the curry, and there was the mincemeat, mixed into the sauce.

'Thank you,' said Nobuo, bowing in his seat.

'Enjoy it while it's hot,' said Nagare. He nodded to Koishi and the two of them withdrew to the kitchen.

'Grandpa, can I start?' Fuminori had already loosened his spoon from the paper napkin, and was holding it at the ready.

'Make sure you say *itadakimasu* first. And it's hot, so blow on it, or you'll burn your mouth.'

Nobuo pressed his own palms together over the table, then reached for his spoon.

Fuminori's eyes sparkled as he followed suit. '*Itadakimasu!*' He began munching away.

'Good?' asked Nobuo.

'Yeah,' said Fuminori through a mouthful of curry. '*So* good. Come on, Grandpa, you try some too!'

'I think I will. Here goes.' Nobuo hastily reached for his spoon and scooped up some of the dark brown sauce and rice.

'Oh . . . it *is* good! *This is it!* This is the curry!'

'Grandpa, do you have to shout like that? It's kind of scary.'

'Oh, er . . . sorry. It's just, it really does taste the same.'

Fuminori's spoon paused on its way to his mouth. 'The same as what?'

'I told you this morning, didn't I? The curry your mother once made me.'

The spoon resumed its motion. 'Oh, right. Well, Mum's curry's the best!'

'He's not as bad as you think, Dad. I'm not asking you to like him. I just wondered if you'd at least show your face at the wedding. I want you to see me in my dress.'

'Yoko . . . it's not too late to call it off. I'll pay the cancellation fee if you like.'

'I know you've never been one to change your mind, but still . . .' said Yoko, her voice trailing off sadly.

'You're one to talk. When was the last time you backed out of anything? You're going to regret this, I swear.'

Even as they spoke, their spoons never stopped moving.

'Tasty, isn't it?' said Yoko, wiping the corner of one eye with her little finger.

'It's fantastic. I hope you're not planning on making this for him.'

Yoko's shoulders sagged with frustration. 'Really can't let it go, can you?'

'This beef is really something.'

'That reminds me. You can't just eat meat, Dad. It's bad for you. At least try a little fish from time to time.'

'I've made it this far, haven't I? At this point, I might as well eat whatever I please.'

A silence descended, broken only by the sounds of their spoons colliding with their plates.

'Well, there we go,' said Yoko when they'd finished. She took the plates over to the sink, where she stood facing away from him.

'Just leave them there. I'll wash them myself. I always do.'

'Can't have my dad cleaning up after me,' said Yoko, and he heard the sound of water running from the tap.

'Yoko.'

The water stopped, and she turned around. 'What, Dad?'

'You can always come back here, you know.'

There was a pause before she replied. 'You raised me to be stronger than that, Dad, and you know it.'

And Yoko set the plates down on the dish rack.

'You okay, Grandpa?'

Fuminori's voice brought Nobuo back to his senses.

'Sorry. It's just . . . so tasty that it seems a shame to finish it!'

'If *you're* not going to eat it, I will.' By this point Fuminori had already polished off a good portion of his curry.

'You're hooked, aren't you? Well, if you like it that much, then how about we just . . .' said Nobuo, and he swapped their plates.

'Anyone for seconds?' Nagare emerged from the kitchen with a silver tray, having apparently noticed what was transpiring. 'There's plenty more in the pot.'

'Mr Kamogawa . . . I know I asked you to recreate the curry, so maybe I shouldn't be so surprised, but . . . how on earth did you pull it off? It tastes *exactly* the same.'

Nagare glanced at Fuminori. 'You two just enjoy your meal for now, and I'll tell you all about it in a moment.'

Nobuo watched Nagare place a second plate of curry in front of Fuminori, then tried some more himself. It really was uncanny. Everything about the curry – not only its appearance, but the tiniest details of its flavour – matched the one Yoko had made him that day.

Was the nostalgia he felt in his chest coming from the curry itself, or his recollection of that last meal with Yoko? Probably both, thought Nobuo. Savouring every mouthful, he carried on munching away until there wasn't a single grain of rice left on his plate.

The second portion must have been slightly smaller than the first, because Fuminori had almost finished that, too.

'Wow,' said Fuminori, setting his spoon back down with a contented look on his face. 'Mum makes *such* good curry.'

'Actually, she didn't make it. The nice man who runs this restaurant made one that tastes just like hers.'

'What, so he copied her?'

'You could put it that way. Your mother made such a

delicious curry that he just couldn't resist trying to make it himself.'

Nagare emerged from the kitchen and refilled their glasses with water.

'It's bad to copy people, you know,' Fuminori declared. 'But since it was so tasty, I'll let you off.'

'Fuminori! Don't be so rude!' Nobuo glared at his grandson, then rose from his seat and bowed apologetically to Nagare. 'Sorry about that.'

Nagare chuckled. 'Oh, not at all. He's right, anyway. It's no good just copying other people's cooking.'

Nobuo drained his glass, then turned in Nagare's direction once more. 'So, care to tell me how you managed it?'

'Fuminori, do you like animals?' cut in Koishi.

The boy's eyes lit up. 'I love them! Like elephants and giraffes and things.'

'How about cats?'

'I like them too. I play with Kazuto's every day.'

'That's his friend who lives two doors down from us,' explained Nobuo. 'He's always going round there to play.'

'Well then,' said Koishi. 'How about you and I go and play with the cat?'

'Okay!' exclaimed Fuminori, hopping down from his chair almost simultaneously.

Nagare waited for the pair to step outside, then sat down opposite Nobuo.

'So I got it just about right, then?'

'Not "just about". It was identical. Looked and tasted *exactly* the same. Feels like I've just seen a magic trick.' Nobuo could barely conceal his astonishment.

'They used to make a curry like this one at a restaurant here in Kyoto. Indika, it was called – a curry specialist, over in Kiyamachi. Closed down five years ago.'

'Indika, eh? Never heard of it. Was it famous here?'

'I think it was the sort of place where if you knew, you knew. I'd heard of it myself, but never got round to going.'

Nobuo leaned forward. 'But why did Yoko . . . ?'

'Mind if I start at the beginning?'

'Please,' said Nobuo, sitting up straight to listen.

'My first port of call was the cafeteria at Yoko's dormitory. I got them to make an exception and let me in. Turns out the head cook remembers Yoko well. Apparently Yoko used to call her "Mum" as a kind of joke. She told me all sorts about your daughter's student days.'

'I do remember her mentioning someone who was like a mother to her. That must have been her.' Nobuo frowned. 'Bet she wasn't very impressed by Yoko's choice of boyfriend.'

'Yep. She saw it the same way you did. Couldn't fathom why an intelligent young woman like Yoko would ever fall for someone like that. This is the part I didn't want

Fuminori to hear, see. Even at his age, no kid wants to hear their father spoken of that way.'

'Appreciate you being so considerate. I should probably watch what I say about him too.'

'Anyway, it seems her boyfriend was pretty strapped for cash. Could barely afford his university fees. Yoko was so moved by his plight that she started working part-time as a home tutor in order to help him out.'

'See, I just can't get my head around that,' said Nobuo coldly.

'Next, I visited the house where she used to tutor. The Ishihara family.'

'You really have been running all over the place, haven't you?'

'At the time, the girl she was teaching was in her fifth year of primary school. Her mother had nothing but good things to say about Yoko. "Always so diligent and polite," were her words.'

'Well, I was pretty strict with her on both those fronts,' said Nobuo proudly.

'They were still short of money, so she started working part-time at the weekends, too. At that Indika place I just mentioned.'

'So *that's* how she learned to make the curry.'

'She was there for two years – more than enough time to pick up the recipe, even just by watching.'

'But if the place no longer exists, how did you manage to . . . ?'

'It was Mrs Ishihara who got Yoko that job at Indika. The woman who ran the restaurant was an old school friend of hers. They stayed in touch even after it shut down.'

Nagare paused to drain his glass of water. Nobuo was staring at his mouth, as if willing him to go on.

'I learned from Mrs Ishihara that Indika had a sister restaurant in Himeji, going by the same name, where they were still serving this curry. She put me in touch with its owner.'

'You went all the way to . . . Himeji?'

'Oh, getting there from Kyoto is a breeze on the express train. Bit of a walk from the station, mind . . .' Nagare produced a photo of the Himeji restaurant.

'Looks fancy.'

'For somewhere so out of the way, it was pretty busy. Hardly surprising – this curry of theirs is one of a kind.'

'I definitely wouldn't mind making the trip if I knew a plate of this stuff was waiting for me.'

'The exact recipe is a closely guarded secret – but seeing as I knew Mrs Ishihara, they were kind enough to give me a few hints. That, with a few of Yoko's own twists, resulted in the curry I just served you.'

'Ah. So this wasn't exactly the same as what they served at Indika?' asked Nobuo, gesturing at his empty plate.

'See, Yoko was concerned you weren't eating enough

fish, so she had a word with that head cook at the cafeteria. Asked her if she could think of any way of smuggling some into your food.'

Nobuo's eyes widened. 'There was . . . fish in it?'

'One of the tricks at Indika is that they add a tiny bit of soy sauce to the curry to lift the flavour. But Yoko went further: she added some seasoned minced bonito. What you thought was mincemeat was actually minced fish. And in the original Indika curry, there was no mince of any sort.'

'Bonito? Really?'

'Yoko even wrote to the cook to tell her how well her advice had worked – that her curry-loving father had wolfed it down.'

'I see,' murmured Nobuo. His voice was trembling with emotion. 'Well, now I know why she made curry, of all things.'

'A sort of present for you, I guess. Before she got married.'

'Mr Kamogawa . . .'

'Yes?'

A faint shimmer had appeared in Nobuo's eyes. 'Do you think I . . . did the wrong thing? Should I have turned up at her wedding, even if I couldn't bear to watch her marry him?'

'Listen, I'm just an old codger running a restaurant.

Hardly in any position to be lecturing anyone on whether they did the right thing. But I'm also father to a daughter. And whatever happens down the line, I trust Koishi's judgement. If she picks herself a husband, then I'm prepared to accept him – no matter what sort of man he is.' Nagare said these last words with assurance.

'Guess I ought to have done the same, then.'

'Maybe it's like I was saying about food. You can't rank people from best to worst. They don't come in different grades. They're all just people.'

'So that's where I went wrong.'

'I keep telling you, it's not about being right or wrong . . . Anyway, you got yourself an adorable little grandson into the bargain. And when Yoko does come home, you'll have your chance to start things over with her.'

Nagare was looking him right in the eye. Nobuo didn't stir an inch.

'You about done in here?' asked Koishi, peering in through the door she'd just half opened.

'*You about done in here?*' repeated Fuminori in his best imitation of her Kyoto accent, as he stuck his head around the door below her.

'Good timing. In you come. Your father here was just saying it was time for you to be heading home.'

Nobuo got to his feet and bowed deeply. 'Thank you for everything.'

Fuminori ran to his side and followed suit, adding a 'Thank you!' of his own.

'Your manners really are something else, aren't they?' said Nagare, patting him on the head. As Fuminori burrowed shyly into his grandfather's side, Koishi presented him with a white paper bag.

'This is for you to take home. So that your grandfather can make that curry for you again sometime.'

'Thank you,' said Nobuo. 'Now, let me pay for everything.' He got out his wallet.

'How about we call it even?' said Nagare. 'Seeing as I owe you for those bowls, I mean.'

'You really don't mind? A few bowls hardly feels like enough to cover it.'

'Really, it's fine.'

'Alright then, if you insist.' Nobuo pressed his palms together in gratitude.

'There's a jar of the curry in there – as well as a simple version of the recipe. I'm sure your grandson would love it if you made it for him.'

Hearing this, Fuminori peered excitedly into the bag.

As Koishi slid the door open, Drowsy greeted them with a soft mewl. Nobuo stepped outside, then turned and bowed.

'This has really helped, you know.'

Fuminori was gazing up at Koishi. 'Hey, Mum, can we

come back some time?' He stopped, mortified by what he'd said. 'Oh. Sorry . . . I meant to say Koishi.'

'I can't believe you even have to ask!' exclaimed Koishi, instinctively hugging the young boy tight. Even Drowsy was nuzzling his legs. 'You're *always* welcome, you hear?'

'I'll be wishing your daughter a speedy return home,' said Nagare.

Nobuo bowed deeply in response.

Clearly reluctant to part ways, Fuminori kept turning and waving. Every time he did so, Nobuo would turn, too, and give another quick bow.

Their two long shadows grew smaller and smaller, until they disappeared entirely from view.

'Sad old story, wasn't it?' said Koishi when they were back inside.

'That's life for you, I guess. A crime's a crime, whatever the circumstances. Always a price to be paid.'

'Well, yeah, but . . .'

'She'll be out of there soon enough, Koishi.'

Nagare kneeled in front of the family altar and lit a stick of incense. Koishi came to join him, pensively pressing her hands together.

'Mum, pray for her to be released as soon as possible, okay?'

'I know it seems tough,' said Nagare, 'but at least she's

still alive, and Nobuo still gets to see her. Could be worse.'
He glanced up the altar. 'Couldn't it, Kikuko?'

'I wonder what *my* mum's curry tasted like.'

'Wasn't her forte, let's put it that way,' replied Nagare with a smile. 'You could hardly call it curry, it was that mild.'

Koishi, too, was gazing up at the altar.

'Mild would be fine with me. I just wish I could try it.'

Chapter 3:
Yakisoba

1

Just across Karasuma-dori from Higashi Honganji temple is Shomen-dori – a narrower street lined with shops selling altar fittings, religious clothing and other Buddhist supplies. That afternoon, a taxi was moving down it at a leisurely pace, heading west.

A pair of young women in summer kimonos, each twirling a paper parasol, caught the driver's eye.

Occupying the middle of the back seat, meanwhile, was Yumiko Maezaki. Clad in a tight-fitting trouser suit, she was leaning forward, one hand resting on the driver's seat.

'You sure it's around here?' he asked impatiently, glancing left and right as he adjusted his grip on the wheel. 'I can't see anything that looks like a restaurant.'

'I'm sure of it. Look, the map says so.' Yumiko bent forward even further and showed him the map in question.

'Well, maybe there's something wrong with your map.

I've been driving this taxi for years, and I've never heard of anywhere like that around here.'

'There, on the left,' said Yumiko, pointing at a two-storey mortar-clad building. 'That could be it, don't you think?'

'Looks like someone's house, if you ask me. There isn't even a sign.'

'Yes, but I've heard it's that sort of place. This has to be it.' A note of certainty had entered Yumiko's voice. 'Can I get out here, please?'

'Be my guest,' said the driver, reluctantly applying the brakes. 'But I really don't think—'

'Don't worry about the change. Just open the door, please!'

The fare was 610 yen, and Yumiko had just handed the driver a thousand-yen note.

'You young ladies really don't have time to lose, do you?' said the driver, chuckling as he folded up the banknote.

'Actually, I'm almost forty.'

For all the alacrity with which Yumiko jumped out of the taxi, clutching her small, wheeled suitcase, she found herself hesitating in front of the building, as though slightly thrown by its appearance.

It really didn't look like much of a restaurant. But that was definitely the smell of food wafting from the door.

Yumiko adjusted the collar of her jacket, clenched her fists, and muttered, 'Here we go.' She slid the door open.

'Hello there!'

It was a more cheerful greeting than she'd been expecting. Yumiko felt a wave of relief as she turned to the young woman who had issued it. Dabbing at the sweat on her forehead with a lace handkerchief, she asked, 'Is this the Kamogawa Diner?'

'It is, but . . . are you just here to eat?'

Yumiko felt another jolt of anxiety. Maybe she was less welcome than she'd thought.

'Actually, I'd like your help in tracking down a certain dish . . .'

'Ah, you're one of *those*. I'm Koishi Kamogawa – in charge of the detective agency.'

'Yumiko Maezaki. Pleased to meet you.' She presented her business card.

'Head of the Maezaki Foundation . . .' read Koishi. 'What sort of work is that, then?'

Before she could reply, a chef appeared from the kitchen, removed his hat and bowed.

'Thank you for making the trip. Nagare Kamogawa – in charge of the restaurant. This is my daughter.'

'It's a pleasure. I actually only got back to Japan ten days ago.' Yumiko handed Nagare a leaflet of some kind, which he received with elaborate gratitude.

'Always so busy, aren't you?' he said. 'It's such wonderful work that you do.'

Koishi looked on in bewilderment as the two carried on like old friends.

'So, where are you off to this time?' asked Nagare.

'Tochigi. The area affected by the flooding.'

'Ah. I'm sure they'll be delighted to have you. The first time you did this was after the Kobe earthquake, wasn't it?'

'That's right. It was my father who came up with the idea.'

'He didn't come with you this time, then?'

'He passed away two years ago, sadly.'

'Really. I'm sorry to hear that.'

With their game of conversational catch showing no sign of letting up, Koishi decided to intervene. 'You must be hungry. Can we get you something to eat?'

Yumiko smiled. 'If you're serving food, that would be wonderful.'

'Anything you don't eat?' asked Nagare.

'No, though sometimes I wish there was. It's the sort of thing that intrigues people, isn't it?' She flashed Nagare a teasing glance as he made his way into the kitchen.

'Watch out,' said Koishi, casting a disapproving glance in her father's direction. 'He has a soft spot for pretty young women like you.'

'I'm in my late thirties. Is that "young" in Japan these days?' said Yumiko, settling into a chair.

Koishi paused in the middle of wiping down the table. 'Oh. We're about the same age, then.'

'Really?' said Yumiko, smiling faintly. 'You don't look a day over thirty.'

'You've certainly got me beat in the charm department,' said Koishi, folding up her cloth more vigorously than seemed necessary.

'You're the one who helps track down the dishes, then?'

'Actually, I just do the initial interview. Dad does the real detective work.'

'I see.' Yumiko's features creased with what looked like relief.

'You live in . . . Australia?' asked Koishi, peering at the address on the business card.

'Austria,' replied Yumiko, a slight edge coming into her voice.

'Oops.' Koishi rubbed her eyes. 'My vision isn't what it used to be . . . Anyway, how did you find out about us?'

'I'm a bit of a foodie, so I have *Gourmet Monthly* sent over from Japan. I spotted your advert in it.'

'But . . . it doesn't give an address or anything, does it?'

'I wrote to the editor, asking her to spill the beans.'

Koishi's shoulders sank slightly. 'I knew it . . .'

'I'd heard Kyoto was hot in the summer, but this is something else, isn't it?'

'Sorry, our air conditioner's not in great shape,' said

Koishi, fiddling with the remote control. 'Dad keeps saying we need to buy a new one.'

'I meant outside. But it is a lovely city. They were play-ing the Gion Festival music at the station, and there were all these young ladies walking around in yukata. The streets are the picture of Japanese summer.'

'Good season for eating, too,' said Nagare, arriving with a large tray full of food.

'Oh my!' exclaimed Yumiko, her eyes flitting between the numerous dishes on the tray. 'I don't know if I can manage all those.'

'Looks like a lot, I know, but they're just little morsels, really. You'll be fine.'

Nagare laid an indigo cloth over the table, then set about arranging the food on it. Each dish elicited a little gasp of appreciation from Yumiko.

'A selection of smaller plates and bowls. The cut-glass bowl in the top left is jellied hamo eel, sprinkled with grated yuzu peel. Next to it, on the Imari dish, is grilled unagi eel – enjoy that with the wasabi soy sauce. To the right of that, in the bamboo basket, are today's deep-fried dishes: Kamo aubergine and Omi beef, both good with a dab of the spicy miso. On the glass plate below that is horsehair crab, topped with a vinegar and soy sauce gelée. The Oribe dish next to that is grilled ayu fry – sprinkle over a bit of the water-pepper vinegar and eat them from the head down. And to the left of that, in the lacquered bowl, is ground edamame, seasoned and mixed with broth – a sort of Japanese-style vichyssoise, if you like. The Kutani bowl below that is locally reared chicken grilled with Takagamine green peppers, in a ponzu dressing. Next to that, on the Shigaraki-ware plate, is steamed abalone in a sauce made from its liver. And the glass bowl in the bottom right is chilled tofu, to be eaten with the olive oil and salt.'

Yumiko nodded vigorously along to this explanation.

'How about something to drink?' asked Koishi.

'Don't suppose you have any sparkling wine?'

'No champagne, I'm afraid,' said Nagare, 'but I do have some spumante. A decent cava, too. You'd prefer something dry, I'm guessing?'

'I would indeed. I'll try the cava.'

'Nothing like a glass of sparkling wine on a summer's day, is there?'

'Actually, I drink it all year round,' replied Yumiko nonchalantly.

Koishi looked at her in amazement. 'Wow, life abroad really is something else. Wish *I* could drink champagne every day.'

'I didn't say champagne! And a lot of sparkling wine isn't much different from table wine.'

'Oh. Is champagne really that much of a cut above the rest?' asked Koishi.

'Well, it's the fact that—'

'Don't worry, I'll school Koishi on the distinction later,' interrupted Nagare, shooting his daughter a look as he set a flute glass down on the table. 'You just relax and enjoy your meal, alright?'

Yumiko was surveying the table with a smile on her face.

'Wouldn't think she worked in a restaurant, would you . . .' Nagare grumbled to her as he smoothly uncorked the bottle.

'Actually, I'm in charge of the detective agency, remember?' said Koishi, huffily turning aside.

Nagare smiled ironically at Yumiko. 'I sometimes wonder if she'll *ever* grow up.'

'Oh, there's nothing wrong with a bit of youthful exuberance,' replied Yumiko, sipping from the flute.

'Well, enjoy! I'll bring the rice through a little later.' Nagare left the wine bottle in an ice bucket on the table, then made his way back into the kitchen, followed by Koishi.

Where to start? Yumiko pondered the question for some time before finally extending her chopsticks in the direction of the horsehair crab, smearing it with the gelée, and slipping it into her mouth. It had all the refreshing sweetness you'd expect of crab in the summer. Vienna offered no shortage of places that served Japanese food – hotel restaurants, for one. But the flavours never quite matched the ones she carried in her memory. Of course, her real purpose in returning to Japan was to give classes in disaster-stricken areas – to bring a smile to the faces of afflicted residents, and children in particular. But she couldn't deny that the prospect of enjoying the country's food again was something she always looked forward to immensely.

I've been here for ten days now, but this is the first time I've eaten real Japanese food, she thought as she bit into one of the grilled ayu fry.

And nothing said 'summer in Kyoto' as much as jellied hamo eel – or so she'd been led to believe by various guidebooks. She carried on nibbling away at the dishes in front of her, pausing every now and then for a sip of cava. When she'd finished about half of them, Nagare returned from the kitchen.

'All alright?' There was a gentle hissing and fizzing as he refilled her glass.

'You know, I'd forgotten just how delicious Japanese food can be. I'm always eating pale imitations of it, you see. This is the real deal.'

'It's not like I trained under a master chef or anything, so these are all just experiments really. I don't know if you can call it traditional Japanese cuisine in the proper sense. Still, I'll admit it probably tastes better than some of those "modern Japanese" places that seem to be all the rage these days.'

'It's only been about three years since I was last in the

country, but it does seem like a lot of chefs these days think it's all about putting on a show – at the expense of actual flavour . . .'

'I bet an artist like you can see right through that sort of showboating. I couldn't agree more – it's the customer who's supposed to be in the limelight, not the chef. My boss always used to say the same thing: chefs don't know how to serve their customers any more. These days, they think it's all about them.'

Yumiko drained her glass in one gulp. 'Exactly. The idea that *they* should get to decide everything – even how quickly you eat!'

'I mean, I do ask first-time customers to leave the menu up to me,' said Nagare as he refilled her glass, 'but my regulars can order whatever they like.'

Yumiko reached for one of the deep-fried chunks of aubergine with her fingers. 'Open up a branch in Vienna, would you?'

'I'd have to run that past Koishi,' replied Nagare with a grin. 'Enjoy the rest of your meal – and let me know when you'd like that rice.' He bowed and withdrew once more.

By now the bottle of cava was two thirds empty. Yumiko's chopsticks glided steadily back and forth as she tried the abalone, unagi and chilled tofu, each of which induced a smile of pleasure. Just as Nagare had predicted, she was going to have no problem finishing her meal. When she was almost done she called out to him. He appeared a moment later bearing a bowl of rice topped with eel.

'Thought I'd grill some soy-marinated hamo eel, rather than the usual unagi. Steamed it too, Tokyo-style, so the bones should be nice and soft. This soup is made from the liver – add a dash of ginger juice if you feel like it. As for the eel, some of this ground sansho pepper should pair with it nicely.'

The contents of the blue-and-white porcelain bowl looked identical to when the dish was made with unagi eel. Smelled pretty similar, too. She fished out a piece of the hamo, sprinkled it liberally with the sansho pepper, then used it to scoop up some of the sauce-infused rice before popping the whole thing into her mouth. The rice was much hotter than it had appeared, causing Yumiko to cough slightly at first, but soon she was chewing away with a blissful smile on her face.

She removed the lid from the soup bowl, unleashing a swirl of steam. Without hesitation, she poured the small cup of ginger juice into the bowl, then slowly brought it to her lips. There was none of the pronounced smell usually associated with liver, and the broth – presumably also drawn from the hamo – was so rich in flavour as to be almost sensuous.

'Some hojicha.' Nagare set down a Mino-ware clay teapot full of the roasted green tea, together with a tall teacup. 'There's plenty more rice if you feel like it, by the way.'

'I've eaten so much already,' said Yumiko, a slight blush rising to her cheeks. 'Can't even remember the last time I had this much. And there I was saying I didn't think I'd finish it – sorry!'

'Don't apologize,' smiled Nagare. 'Polishing off a meal like that is the biggest compliment you can pay the chef.'

'I'm glad you see it that way. If my father had seen me pigging out like this, he'd have given me a real earful.'

'I guess living abroad only made him even more determined to raise you the old-fashioned way.'

'And if I ever complained about the slightest thing, he'd really flip. Even when I was little.'

'Must have been tough, everyone calling you a prodigy from such an early age,' said Nagare, pouring the last of the cava into her glass. 'No wonder you gave up playing while you were still young.'

Yumiko simply sighed, but she appeared to be blinking back tears.

'Sorry for talking your ear off,' said Nagare. 'Koishi's waiting in the office. Shall I show you through to her?'

Yumiko responded with a brief nod.

Nagare led her down a long, narrow corridor. Perhaps because of all the cava, she was a little unsteady on her feet, her head drooping as she trudged along behind him. Nagare glanced back over his shoulder, slowing his pace to match hers.

'You alright?'

'Sorry.' Yumiko sighed deeply as she came to a halt. 'I might have had a little too much to drink.'

'Don't worry about it. You could always tell us about this dish you're looking for another time.'

Yumiko shook her head vigorously. 'That's very kind of you. But I'd rather it was today.' She patted her face vigorously, then began walking again.

'I'll let Koishi take it from here, then.' Nagare opened the door to the office, then retreated down the corridor.

After slowly filling out the form Koishi handed her, Yumiko slid it back across the table separating them.

'Yumiko Maczaki,' read Koishi. 'Thirty-eight years old. Piano teacher. Ah, so you teach?'

Yumiko gazed up at the ceiling. 'These days, yes.'

'You did something else before, then?'

'I was a pianist.'

'Ah. The same line of work.'

'Actually, it's completely different,' said Yumiko, flushing slightly. 'An athlete in her prime isn't exactly the same as one who's given up her sport for good, is she?'

'Sorry . . . my mistake.' Startled, Koishi decided to change the subject. 'What's this dish you're looking for, then?'

'Yakisoba,' replied Yumiko, her voice growing distant.

'Right. When and where did you eat it?'

'Fifteen years ago, in Osaka.'

'Phew! I was thinking we might have to go all the way to Australia.'

'*Austria.*'

Koishi flinched visibly. 'Sorry. Could you tell me a little bit more about this yakisoba, then?' She opened up her notebook and clicked her pen.

'Well, someone cooked it for me, but it was just an ordinary yakisoba, really. With the usual sauce.'

'You mean, like the type you'd get at an okonomiyaki place?' asked Koishi, who was already sketching an illustration in her notebook.

'We moved to Austria when I was eight, and I've only been back a few times since, so I don't have much to compare it to. But I remember having some when I was still in nursery school, from a stall at a festival – and it was a lot like that.'

'Right. So, completely ordinary yakisoba, with no distinguishing features.' Koishi sighed. 'These are always the hardest ones . . . Was there really nothing at all that stood out about it? Even the tiniest detail would help.'

'It looked . . . pretty normal, I'd say,' said Yumiko, her gaze drifting across the ceiling as she recalled the dish in question. 'The noodles were this dark brown colour, but they weren't that heavily flavoured. There was a fried egg on top, and shreds of red pickled ginger on the side.'

'That does all sound pretty standard . . . What else was in it?'

'Thin slices of pork belly, beansprouts, negi onion. I think that was it.'

'No cabbage?'

'Not that I recall. It's all a little hazy . . .'

'What about the flavour? Just your usual Worcestershire-style sauce?'

'Again, my memory might be playing tricks on me, but I remember it tasting slightly of dashi stock.'

'Right. And not because it had bonito flakes on top?'

'No, there was no bonito, as far as I can remember.'

'That sounds like a useful hint.' Koishi scribbled something down in her notebook.

'Oh yes. The other thing I found odd was that, after bringing it to the table, the man who cooked it recommended adding a bit of extra sauce.'

'Maybe it was under-seasoned?'

'Maybe. But the sauce was on the table right from the start. It's not like he only brought it over afterwards.'

'Right. And . . . you mentioned a man just now, didn't you?'

'I did.' Yumiko blushed and lowered her gaze to the table.

'If you're comfortable sharing,' said Koishi, peering intently at her, 'would you mind telling me about him?'

'Fifteen years ago, I did a month-long tour of the Kansai area, playing benefit concerts for victims of the Kobe earthquake. He was the tour manager.'

'Can you tell me his name?'

'Toru Sugahara.'

'And how old were you both at the time?'

'I was twenty-three. He's two years older than me, so he would have been twenty-five.'

'And where did he make you this yakisoba?'

'The hotel in Osaka where I was staying. My room was one of the ones for longer stays, with a kitchenette. That's where he made it.'

'Osaka, eh?' said Koishi as she jotted this down. 'If there was ever a city to eat yakisoba in . . .'

'Is Osaka famous for it? I was born in Tokyo, so I wouldn't know too much about that. In fact, even when I stayed there, I don't think I ate much that counted as proper Osaka food.'

'Did you eat out a lot?'

'Oh yes. All I used the kitchenette for was coffee and toast in the morning. The rest of the time it was one government official or sponsor after another inviting me out for lunch or dinner.'

'I imagine that got pretty tiring in its own way. Eating at restaurants all the time.'

'Yes – and having to constantly make conversation . . . That probably sounds ungrateful of me.'

'No, I get it.'

'Anyway, Toru was kind enough to keep my last night in Japan free.'

'And you had yakisoba for your last meal in the country? Pretty unusual choice . . .'

'He insisted,' said Yumiko, a distant look coming into her eyes. 'Said he really wanted to make it for me.'

'Mind if I ask a slightly personal question?'

'What would that be?'

'Was all this . . . strictly professional?'

'Lying won't do me any good, will it? Yes, we were . . . seeing each other, I suppose you'd say. Not that it lasted very long.' Yumiko blushed. 'He was my first love.'

'I knew it! I mean, the fact that he was in your hotel room sort of gave it away . . .' Koishi let her words hang in the air.

'After we moved to Austria, I spent all my days at the piano. I didn't even have *time* to fall in love. My parents were both musicians, so it wasn't like they were out at work every day, either. They barely let me out of their sight.'

'I guess they wanted to shelter you. Speaking of which . . . they must have been anxious about you coming to Japan on your own?'

'They called me at least three times a day.'

'But you fell in love anyway. I guess there isn't much that can get in the way of that.'

'I had no idea how to even act around men – and yet every minute with him felt like a dream.' Yumiko sat up slightly on the sofa. 'He gave me the strength to keep performing every day, too.'

'And why did Mr Sugahara want to cook you yakisoba, of all things?'

'Well, it was a favourite of his. His . . . comfort food, I guess you'd say.'

'Did it have some sort of special meaning for him, do you think?' asked Koishi as she began sketching again.

'I'm not sure. But he did seem very surprised that I liked it so much. Kept asking me if I really meant it. I told him there wouldn't be much point in me lying!'

'You said it was his comfort food. Is that how he described it himself?'

'He didn't use that phrase, no. But he did tell me that yakisoba had always been his go-to – both when he was feeling down, and when something good had happened.'

'In which case . . . I wonder if it was a local speciality where he was from. Do you know where he grew up?'

'Somewhere up north, he said. I'm not sure exactly where, though.'

'Did he have an accent or anything?'

'No, he spoke standard Japanese.'

'And seeing as you're here asking us to find this dish, I'm guessing you haven't stayed in touch?'

'That's right,' replied Yumiko in a low voice.

Koishi clicked her pen a few times, then looked up at Yumiko. 'So . . . what exactly made you want to eat the yakisoba again, after all this time?'

Yumiko's expression stiffened slightly.

'. . . Not that you have to tell me, if you'd rather not.'

Yumiko sighed, gazing vacantly at the table. She was sitting perfectly still.

A silence settled over the room until, with apparent reluctance, Yumiko broke it.

'I want to go back.'

'Go . . . back?' repeated Koishi, sitting up to listen.

'My life changed for ever that day. Even if I can't actually travel back in time, I'd like to at least remember how I felt.'

'A plate of yakisoba changed your life?'

'I was head over heels. I'd never really been in love at all before – and now that it had finally happened, I was completely defenceless. I got it into my head that I could stay in Japan to be with him.'

'You really fell for him, then.' Koishi sank slightly in her seat. 'Wish I knew what that felt like . . .'

'I think it was mutual. But Toru was the cautious type,

and at some point he got cold feet. I was beginning to make quite a name for myself, and he kept saying it wouldn't be right to keep me all to himself . . . Meanwhile, there I was, desperately wishing he'd whisk me away. It was so frustrating.'

'I'd give anything to fall in love like that. Just once.'

Yumiko didn't seem to hear her. 'It dawned on me that if I gave up the piano, there'd be nothing to keep us apart.' She paused. 'You know, I ate that yakisoba with a fork. I was useless with chopsticks back then.'

'You seemed pretty handy with them just now in the restaurant.'

'When you're a pianist, your fingers are everything. My parents seem to have decided it would be safer if I stuck with forks, which I'd grown used to in Austria. So even when we had Japanese food at home, they'd make me use a fork.'

'You pianists really don't have it easy.'

'I was tired of doing every little thing they told me. It just felt so pointless. Even if I'd told them about Toru, they never would have allowed it. I knew that unless I did something, I'd end up living my whole life as a sort of robot controlled by my parents.'

'So you decided to throw a spanner in the works.'

'I told myself that if I could just shed my identity as a pianist, my parents would stop trying to control me. In other words, all I needed to do was ensure I couldn't play any more.'

'No . . .' murmured Koishi, her eyes widening anxiously. 'You don't mean . . .'

'I gave him the fork, held out the back of my hand and told him to stab it.'

Koishi shuddered visibly. 'Talk about desperate measures!'

'I just wanted to be with him.' Yumiko was stroking the back of her left hand. 'That was all I could think of.'

'And did he . . . do it?' asked Koishi, leaning forward.

'He did. Only hard enough to leave a slight graze, mind. The sight of the blood sent him into a panic. He started crying, apologizing over and over for what he'd done, then ran right out of the room.'

'Still, I can't believe he actually went through with it!'

'Only because I kept begging him to. I told him that if he really loved me, he'd stab me.'

'What happened after that?'

'That was the last time I ever saw him. He didn't even see me off at the airport.'

'And that injury was the reason you stopped performing?'

'He probably thinks it was. The truth is I stabbed my hand again myself afterwards – harder this time.' She showed Koishi the faint scar that remained on her hand.

'*This* was enough to stop you from playing?' asked Koishi, taking her hand and inspecting it closely.

'Oh, I could still get the notes out,' said Yumiko, stroking the scar again. 'But as a professional, I was finished. My skin never regained its flexibility, and the subtlety of my playing went out the window.'

'It's like the plot of some tragedy. Your parents must have been devastated.'

'They couldn't even process it. Both of them spent the next six months or so in a deep depression. The only ray of hope that shone into our house was when I started to find work teaching the piano instead of playing it.'

'Your pupils must have been thrilled to have *you* teaching them. From concert pianist to teacher – it's quite the story . . .'

'People said all sorts of things, of course. I kept insisting it was an accident, but there were even rumours I'd been trying to take my own life.'

'Just because you're famous, people think they can say whatever they like, don't they?'

Yumiko let out a deep sigh. 'Looking back, I can see how reckless youth makes us. How it messes with our judgement.'

'Say we manage to find this yakisoba of yours, and all those emotions come rushing back to you. What do you plan to do then?'

'The truth is . . . I've fallen in love with someone else. A little embarrassing at my age, I know.'

'Oh, not at all. Wonderful. Are you planning on getting married?'

'My parents have passed away now, so I do feel a little freer. There's that, and the fact that I've been a little lonely. So yes, we're going to tie the knot.'

'And before that, you want to eat the yakisoba. Is that so you can make a clean break with the past?' asked Koishi, scribbling away in her notebook.

Yumiko's expression turned distant. 'I suppose I just want to understand how I feel about it all.'

'Got it,' said Koishi, closing her notebook. 'I'll get Dad on the case.'

When they returned to the restaurant, Nagare peered out from the kitchen.

'How was that, then?'

'I got all the details, Dad.'

Yumiko bowed to them both. 'I really appreciate you giving me the chance to talk about all this.'

'We'll do everything we can to find this dish you're after,' said Nagare. 'But I'm guessing you're on a bit of a tight schedule?'

'I'm in the country for another two weeks or so. If you could manage it by then, I'd be very grateful.'

'I'll leave no stone unturned,' said Nagare as he emerged from the kitchen. 'Not that I know what I'm looking for yet,' he added with a chuckle.

'You better had, Dad. Her future happiness is at stake!'

Nagare's brow furrowed slightly. 'You don't need to spell it out for me.'

'Thank you so much,' said Yumiko. 'Now, I still owe you for lunch.'

'We'll take payment for that later on,' explained Koishi. 'Together with the detective fee.'

'I see. Then I'll be looking forward to hearing from you. My number's on the business card I gave you.'

'Got it,' said Nagare, eyeing the card in question.

'Will you be alright on your own?' asked Koishi.

'Oh yes,' said Yumiko as she stepped out of the restaurant, gripping the handle of her suitcase. 'I'm staying at a hotel by the station tonight. It'll be a nice walk.'

'It's hot out here,' said Nagare, shielding his eyes from the sun. 'You take care, okay?'

Yumiko glanced up and down Shomen-dori. 'Which way was the station again?'

'Straight down here,' explained Nagare, pointing, 'then south along Karasuma-dori. Just head for Kyoto Tower and you can't go wrong.'

'Thank you very much. I'll be looking forward to next time.'

Rolling her suitcase behind her, Yumiko set off down the street.

'So, what's she looking for?' asked Nagare when they were back inside.

'Yakisoba.'

'Right. As in . . . yakisoba?'

'As in, yakisoba.'

'You know, we have a real flair for communication sometimes.'

Koishi chuckled. 'Wasn't expecting her to come out with a dish like that, though.'

'Me neither. But I'm guessing there's a reason.'

'The dish might be ordinary, but the story behind it . . . I'm telling you, Dad, this one beats any soap opera on TV.'

Nagare snorted in amusement. '*You*'ve also got a flair for exaggeration.'

'I'm serious!' Koishi sat down at one of the tables and flipped open her notebook. 'You're not even going to believe it at first.'

Nagare sat down opposite her. 'Go on, then. I'm all ears.'

2

With her schedule filling up rapidly ahead of her departure from Japan, Yumiko had somehow managed to keep this one afternoon free.

Leaving Kyoto station via the Karasuma exit, she headed north, her feet almost moving of their own accord. In no time at all, she had turned east onto Shomen-dori and found herself standing in front of the Kamogawa Diner.

Mrrrow.

Yumiko looked down to find a tabby cat weaving between her legs. She crouched and gave it a gentle stroke.

'We call him Drowsy,' said Koishi, sliding the door open and arriving at Yumiko's side. 'All he ever seems to want is a good snooze.'

'Drowsy, eh? Well, *someone's* got it easy.'

'Sorry to invite you back at the last minute like this.'

'Not at all – thanks for making it happen. I've been very excited.'

Yumiko got to her feet. She was clutching a red tote bag.

'I just hope Dad got it right . . .' murmured Koishi nervously.

'Hello again!' Nagare called as they stepped inside.

Yumiko bowed. 'Sorry for putting you to such trouble.'

'I think I've just about cracked it – but my apologies if it's not quite right.'

She nodded in response.

'Please, take a seat,' said Koishi, pulling out one of the folding chairs at a nearby table and pouring her some tea.

Glancing around the restaurant again, memories of the meal she'd had last time came flooding back. It had seemed completely out of keeping with the plain-looking surroundings in which it had been served. Yumiko recalled her father telling her one evening that in Japan people liked to explain these sorts of bewildering situations by claiming they'd been bewitched by a fox.

Maybe, she thought, the very existence of this restaurant was an illusion of that sort. In fact, maybe everything up to this point had just been a sort of dream. Even if it was, though, that was fine by her. After all, wouldn't that make this a fresh start?

'Can I get you something to drink?' asked Koishi.

'Just this tea will be fine,' replied Yumiko with a smile. 'Can't go getting tipsy again.'

'The food should be ready in just a moment,' said Koishi, before hurrying into the kitchen.

How was she supposed to react if they'd got it wrong? And if they'd got it *right* – how would she feel then? Just thinking about it was enough to send a tremor of anticipation through her chest. She reminded herself to take deep breaths.

Maybe she should just claim that something urgent had come up, and make a swift exit.

The truth was, there was another reason for her hesitation. Namely, that she'd invented that story about a fiancé.

'Sorry for the wait.' Nagare had arrived with the yakisoba on a silver tray. There was no going back now. Yumiko sat up in her chair.

'I gave it my best shot. I'll leave the sauce here, so you can add as much of it as you like.' He set a plate piled high with yakisoba down on the table, together with a fork and the bottle of sauce.

'Some water – and a flask for refills,' said Koishi, placing another tray at Yumiko's right.

'Enjoy,' said Nagare, and the pair disappeared back into the kitchen.

Yumiko gazed steadily at the yakisoba for some time, then reached apprehensively for her fork. She twirled some of the dark brown noodles onto it, spaghetti-style, then slid it into her mouth.

'. . . Oh my.'

She had murmured the exact same words, in exactly the same way, all those years ago.

The plate of yakisoba was topped with a fried egg, and here and there she could make out a smattering of negi onion, pork and bean sprouts, but more than anything, it was these dark brown noodles that tasted just as she remembered. Toru had told her to add the sauce before digging in, but she'd insisted on trying a mouthful first. She did the same now. It all came rushing back to her. She could almost see him sitting there opposite her.

Back then, it had only been as she'd pierced the yolk of the egg and smeared it onto the noodles coiled around her fork that the idea had come to her. *If it's this easy to turn the fork yellow, I might as well turn it red.*

Had she really meant to turn her life upside down, or had she just been testing Toru? Seeing how far he'd go for her? Even now, she didn't know. All she knew was that after that plate of yakisoba, things had never been the same again. Lost in these thoughts, Yumiko sat chewing away in silence.

What sort of life had Toru gone on to lead?

The question was enough to make her freeze in the middle of twirling her fork.

'Did I get it right?' asked Nagare, arriving from the kitchen. Yumiko hastily resumed eating.

'From what I can remember, it's pretty much identical.' Her features creased into a smile. 'Looks the same, tastes the same . . .'

'Ah, good. Please, don't slow down on my account,' said Nagare, glancing down at her plate.

She stopped him as he made to leave. 'Sorry, but, erm . . . how did you—'

'You enjoy your noodles, and I'll tell you all about it once you've finished.' With a grin, he slipped back through the curtain and into the kitchen.

It wasn't like she'd had the yakisoba at a restaurant. Instead, Toru, a complete amateur when it came to cooking, had made it for her. It seemed impossible that Nagare could have replicated the dish without somehow talking to him. He must have tracked him down and asked for the recipe in person. Which meant he must know what had become of Toru.

Impatient to hear more, Yumiko wolfed down the rest of the yakisoba, before calling loudly in the direction of the kitchen, 'That was delicious!'

Koishi was there in a flash. 'I'm glad it was just as you remembered.'

'Oh yes. Took me right back.'

'Okay.' Nagare returned with a touchscreen tablet, which he set down on the table. 'About time I showed you how I did it.'

'I'm all ears,' said Yumiko, half rising from her seat in order to bow.

'To be honest,' said Nagare, sitting down opposite her, 'I thought this one was going to be a real headache. But the first clue practically fell into my lap.'

She smiled. 'Oh, good.'

'From what you told Koishi, I had a feeling it might be Ishinomaki yakisoba we were talking about.' Nagare brought up a map on the tablet.

Yumiko's expression clouded over slightly. 'Ishinomaki? Up north? They took a real hit from the tsunami there, didn't they . . .'

'It was the name Sugahara that got me thinking. See, the person credited with inventing Ishinomaki yakisoba is a man from the Fuyumoto noodle company whose name is – you guessed it – Mr Sugahara. Turned out my hunch wasn't wrong. The person who made you these noodles was his son.'

'Really? Ah – but I do remember him saying something about how he'd have to take on the family business one day. I had no idea it would be as a noodle-maker.'

'Around fifteen years ago, Toru Sugahara set up his own yakisoba restaurant. It's in a pretty out-of-the-way spot, plus he refuses media coverage. One of those well-kept secrets.'

Yumiko let out a quiet sigh. 'Fifteen years . . . He opened the restaurant right after we parted, then.'

'I went there and tried the yakisoba,' continued Nagare, bringing up a photo of the restaurant's interior on the tablet. 'He made it right in front of me, so I got a good look at his technique. When I asked, he told me he'd been making it the same way ever since he opened. And that was the yakisoba I just served you.'

'Did you . . . talk to him?'

'Don't worry,' replied Nagare with a smile. 'I didn't give the game away. But he did agree to tell me the whole recipe, right down to the smallest detail.' Nagare began scrolling through a series of photos showing the various stages in the process. 'You use medium-strength wheat flour to make the noodles, and then you steam them. That turns them yellow, a bit like your average Chinese-style noodles, but if you rinse and then steam them *again*, they turn this dark brown colour. It's quite the process. After that, you make the yakisoba the usual way – but just before it's done, you add a bit of dashi stock, put a lid on and quickly fry them in that. Because you've steamed them twice, they absorb plenty of moisture. It's a clever technique. When they finish frying, they're ready to eat – almost. The last part is up to the customer, and that's where this sauce comes in. They add as much or as little as they like – it's all a matter of preference. And that's how Mr Sugahara makes his Ishinomaki yakisoba.'

'Really doesn't cut any corners, does he? No wonder it tastes so good,' Koishi chipped in.

Yumiko leaned forward and gazed happily at the screen. 'Looks like he's doing very well for himself.'

'He did have a sort of glow about him when we chatted. There were plenty of regulars in there, too.'

Yumiko was stroking the back of her hand. 'That's a huge relief to hear.'

'Now you can focus on that fiancé of yours with a clean conscience,' beamed Koishi.

'Ah . . . yes, I suppose I can,' replied Yumiko a little hesitantly.

'Don't imagine the ingredients will be very easy to come by in Austria, but we've written out the recipe for you just in case.' Koishi handed her a plastic folder. 'You can probably get the noodles and sauce sent out to you, at least.'

'Thank you. Now, how much was all this?'

'Our account details are in there, too,' replied Koishi. 'Just send us however much you think it was worth.'

'Got it.' Yumiko slipped the folder into her tote bag, then opened the door to the restaurant.

'Don't even think about it, mister,' said Nagare, shooing Drowsy away from the door. The cat skittered off and hid behind a utility pole, where he sat waiting to see what might transpire.

Koishi narrowed her eyes at him, then turned to Yumiko. 'Dad's always like that with him. The poor thing!'

'Not a cat person, then?' Yumiko asked Nagare.

'It's more the fact that I'm trying to serve people food in there.'

'Right. You have high standards.'

'Got to if you want to make it as a professional, wouldn't you say?'

Yumiko appeared uncertain how to reply.

Nagare produced a leaflet from his pocket and opened it out. 'Looks like the last classes you're giving are the day after tomorrow, up in Utsunomiya?'

'That's right. One in the morning and one in the afternoon. Teaching the kids this and that.'

'If you have a gap in your schedule, you could always pop up to Matsushima for a bit of sightseeing. It's a quick hop on the bullet train.'

'It is, isn't it?' said Yumiko, a knowing twinkle in her eyes.

'They're still recovering from the tsunami up there, but there's plenty of delicious food to be had. Here.' He handed her a data stick. 'I've saved some photos I took on here – as well as a map of all the best restaurants in the region. Including some well-kept secrets.'

Yumiko gazed at him for a moment, then said, 'Well, thank you very much,' and tucked the data stick into her purse.

'Wait, where *is* Matsushima, again?' asked Koishi, crossing her arms.

'You really are hopeless,' said Nagare, grinning ironically at Yumiko, who grinned back.

As she began walking down Shomen-dori, Drowsy mewed in her direction.

'Take care, now!' called Nagare. Yumiko turned, bowed and set off once more.

'Is Matsushima really that special, Dad?' asked Koishi, back in the restaurant.

'Well,' replied Nagare, wiping down the table, 'the bay there is one of the Three Great Sights of Japan. All those islands covered in pine trees. That's got to count for something.'

'Maybe I should go and check it out too, then.'

'You could,' said Nagare as he ducked through the curtain into the kitchen, 'though, unlike our customer just now, you aren't going to find anyone waiting for you.'

'Waiting for me? Hang on . . . what are you . . .' Koishi chased her father into the kitchen.

'Kikuko, help me out here,' said Nagare, lighting a stick of incense at the altar in the adjoining living room. 'Looks like someone's still a bit slow on the uptake. No wonder we still can't find her a match.'

'But, Dad,' said Koishi, planting herself at his side, 'you're always saying your job is finding *food*, not people.'

'Exactly. Yumiko was looking for a certain dish, and I

told her where to find it. What she does next is none of my business.'

'Mum,' said Koishi, joining her hands in prayer, 'you really did marry one of the good ones, didn't you?'

Chapter 4:

Gyoza

1

When Shuji Kosaka stepped off the train and onto platform thirty-one at Kyoto station, he had to physically brace himself against the cold.

At Toyooka, where he'd boarded, the sunshine had been almost spring-like. He'd even pulled his coat off and stuffed it into his small suitcase.

He sat on one of the platform benches, zipped open the suitcase, retrieved the now-crumpled garment and pulled it back on. Then he left the station and walked north up Karasuma-dori. Just after crossing Shichijo-dori, he came to a halt.

He was staring at the menu outside a Chinese-style restaurant. *A gyoza chain? In the heart of Kyoto?* Unable to quite believe it, he reached for his suitcase and carried on walking.

When he and his wife Misako had first come to the

city, just before his university entrance exams, their first port of call had been Higashi Honganji temple. That was almost twenty years ago, and yet the sight of bright yellow leaves from the ginkgo trees planted in front of the temple, whisked up into the air by the cold north wind and carried down Shomen-dori, didn't seem to have changed at all. As though guided by the leaves, Shuji turned east.

Here he was, walking down the same street they'd merrily strolled along all those years ago – and yet now his heart was heavy, as though a mass of air was pressing down on him from above. But the restaurant he was heading to might be able to change all that. Buoyed by this hope, he soon found himself standing in front of a building much like the one he'd been picturing.

But now he was here, he felt a tremor of doubt. There was no sign outside, or any other indication that this was a place of business. He'd been warned it wasn't the most welcoming-looking place, but now he felt positively intimidated.

Shuji cleared his throat loudly as if to expel the tight ball of tension and doubt that had formed in his chest, then slid the door open.

'Hello there!' came the cheerful voice of a woman.

'Is this the Kamogawa Detective Agency – sorry, I mean the Kamogawa Diner?' he asked, closing the door behind him.

'It is,' replied the woman, who was wearing a black sommelier's apron. 'Which one are you after?'

Shuji managed to produce a smile. 'Both, actually.'

'You're hungry, then?' asked the chef, who had just arrived from the kitchen, wiping his hands down on the Japanese-style waist apron he wore over his whites.

'I am,' said Shuji, patting his stomach.

'Then give me a minute and I'll put something together for you. Anything you don't eat?'

'No, I'm fine with anything.' Shuji removed his coat and began looking around as if unsure where to sit.

'Here,' said the woman, gesturing towards a red folding chair at one of the tables. 'Take a seat.'

'Thank you,' said Shuji, before setting his suitcase down on its side and settling into the chair.

'So, where did you hear about us?'

'I saw your advert in *Gourmet Monthly*.'

'And that was enough for you to go on, was it?'

'I got in touch with the editor and asked. She told me I shouldn't miss the chance to try the food, either. So . . . was that Mr Kamogawa just now?'

'The very same. I'm his daughter, Koishi. Technically head of the detective agency.'

'Ah, yes. She mentioned you, too.'

'Where have you come from today, then?' asked Koishi, pouring him some green tea from a Kiyomizu-ware pot.

Shuji reached for the cup of tea. 'Do you know Toyooka? Not too far north-west of here, in Hyogo prefecture.'

'Oh. Is that the place that's famous for those black-and-white storks?'

'That's right. Anything else spring to mind?'

'Hmm . . . Isn't it supposed to get really hot in summer?'

Shuji nodded. 'Correct. There's this hot wind that blows down from the mountains. Storks and hot air – that's about all we've got going for us.' He took a long sip of tea.

Koishi was gazing pensively up at the ceiling. 'I feel like there was something else . . .'

'This, maybe?' said Shuji, turning up his grey sweater to reveal the small blue bag strapped around his waist.

Koishi cocked her head to one side. 'Bags?'

'Yes. Toyooka is supposed to be famous for its bag-making.'

'Right,' replied Koishi, hanging her head apologetically. 'Sorry for not knowing.'

Shuji drained his cup. 'Don't be. All par for the course when you come from a backwater.'

'Are you . . . a bag-maker yourself, then?' Koishi asked, pouring him some more tea.

'Actually, I run a small business hotel. But my wife comes from a family of them.' Shuji patted the bag.

'It's a lovely colour. With those red lines on the blue fabric. Suits you!'

'You think? To be honest, I mainly wear it to keep my wife happy.' He unslung the bag from his waist and tossed it onto the table.

Nagare emerged from the kitchen with a tray full of food.

'Wow,' said Shuji, staring at the tray in wonder. 'Looks like quite the spread!'

'Let me talk you through it,' said Nagare when he'd finished setting out the dishes on the table. 'The fish on the left of the large Tachikui dish is soy-simmered nodoguro. Next to that is duck grilled with rock salt – a cross of wild and domestic breeds. And then Seko crabmeat served in its shell, with a bonito-infused Tosazu vinegar dressing. Below those you have the deep-fried tilefish, with a yuzu and chilli pepper paste. I fried the scales separately, for extra crunch. Next to that, in the small Imari bowl, is a selection of steamed winter vegetables: Kintoki carrot, Shogoin and Sugukina turnips, and red negi onion. Nice with a dab of mustard – a bit like when you have them in oden stew.'

'We never eat anything like this where I'm from. Could I get some sake to go with it?'

'Absolutely,' said Koishi. 'What sort are you after? I could warm it up for you if you like – what with it being so cold at the moment.'

'Do you have anything from Fushimi?'

'How about some cloudy sake from the Tsukino Katsura brewery? Perfect for the season.'

'Sounds ideal.'

As Koishi and Nagare went into the kitchen, Shuji cast his gaze over each of the dishes one more time, then joined his hands together in appreciation.

'I'll leave the bottle with you – drink as much as you'd like!' Koishi had returned with a medium-sized bottle of sake and a Karatsu-ware sake cup, which she deposited on the table before disappearing back through the curtain that led to the kitchen.

Shuji picked up the green bottle and loosened the cap. There was a light pop, indicating that the sake had been fermenting in the bottle.

He filled the large, guinomi-type sake cup to the brim with the cloudy white sake, then immediately took a sip.

The fruity aroma seemed to pass through his mouth before it reached his nose. He felt a slight fizz on his tongue. The sake had been served at room temperature, and yet it warmed him up right away.

'Wow,' he murmured to himself.

He set the cup down, and began his meal with a mouthful of the crabmeat.

A wave of invigorating flavour spread through his mouth. Just the right amount of Tosazu vinegar, too. He could almost smell the sea. He poured himself some more sake.

He moved on to the salt-grilled duck, dabbing it into the fresh wasabi paste it was served with. As he bit into the meat, its juices spilled out onto his tongue – followed by the sharp accent of the wasabi. Again, the sake made for the perfect accompaniment.

He'd never had deep-fried tilefish before, but it paired nicely with the yuzu and chilli pepper paste. The crisply fried scales had a delightful crunch.

Shuji's hotel was a small one, and the only food it served was a simple breakfast, but that still meant he was technically operating within the same industry as this restaurant. The gap between the uninspiring fare he provided and these delectable flavours was so severe as to fill him with something like remorse.

'All okay?' asked Nagare from behind him.

'More than okay. It's incredible.'

'Ah, good. Now, I don't mean to hurry you, but can I bring you the rice? I've made mushi-zushi today.'

Shuji finished pouring himself some more sake, then looked up at Nagare. 'As in, rice steamed with sushi toppings? I've seen it, but never tried it.'

'That's the one. Should be ready in five minutes or so. I'll bring it through nice and hot.'

Shuji watched Nagare return to the kitchen, then took another sip of sake. He was remembering the trip he and Misako had taken to Onomichi, a quaint port town on the Inland Sea, some five years previously.

She'd wanted to try the mushi-zushi, a local speciality,

but he'd found the idea of what was essentially warm sushi thoroughly off-putting. In the end they hadn't gone into the restaurant. After that, a sharpness had hung in the air between them, even as they boarded the cable car that would take them up to the mountain that overlooked the city. Misako had fallen into such a foul mood that the rest of the trip was ruined. In fact, looking back, the incident seemed to mark the exact point at which their relationship had begun to sour. As he waited for the next part of the meal, Shuji felt a bitter taste forming in his mouth.

'Here we are.' Nagare arrived with two lidded bowls on a tray, which he set down on the table.

'This is the . . . erm, mushi-zushi?' Shuji felt a vague pang of disappointment. He had been expecting the rice to come in one of the square wooden steamers he remembered seeing in the window of the Onomichi restaurant.

'I know it might not look it, but this bowl is very hot. I wouldn't touch it unless you want to burn yourself.' Using a dishcloth, Nagare removed the gold-patterned lid from the rice bowl.

It seemed he wasn't exaggerating. A thick column of steam surged up from the bowl, carrying the sweet-and-sour aroma of the seasoned sushi rice to Shuji's nose.

'And this is the soup – tofu cubes in clear broth, with a dash of kudzu starch to thicken it up slightly. Hope it's all to your liking.'

'I could think of nothing better on a cold day like today,' said Shuji, eyes aglow at the sight in front of him.

'I'll bring you some tea through in a moment,' said Nagare, before heading into the kitchen once more.

Call it human nature, but Shuji now had an overwhelming urge to touch the bowl and see just how hot it was. Very, as it turned out. He reached for his earlobe in a folklore-inspired attempt to cool his finger.

The sushi rice was topped with thin strips of omelette, grilled conger eel, steamed prawns, boiled shiitake mushrooms, ginkgo nuts and large green soybeans. There was also a scattering of something reddish-pink – probably dried and shredded fish.

Taking care not to touch the bowl again, Shuji used his chopsticks to scoop up some of the mushi-zushi and slip it into his mouth.

It was so hot that he found himself wondering how it was even possible for food to retain such a high temperature. He opened his mouth wide as he chewed, releasing clouds of steam.

The rice itself was packed with minced conger eel; he could feel its rich umami flavour racing across his tongue. Now he saw what a bit of warmth could bring to a bowl of sushi. If the result was this tasty, then maybe Misako had been right back then, and he ought to have done as she suggested.

Occasionally pausing to cool down, Shuji finished roughly half the bowl before turning his attention to the soup. The tall-sided, lacquered bowl was decorated with inlaid mother-of-pearl and incredibly smooth to the touch, indicating its impeccable craftsmanship.

When he picked it up and removed the lid, a sharp but refreshing aroma rose up to greet him.

'Is that . . . yuzu?' he murmured.

He tilted the bowl towards his mouth, so that the garnish of yellow peel fell onto his tongue. It tasted faintly bitter. The soup had been sitting there for a while now but it, too, was still piping hot.

'Some tea for you,' said Nagare, appearing with a Mashiko-ware clay pot which he placed on the table together with a Tobe-ware cup. As he was making his way back to the kitchen, Shuji called out to him.

'Sorry, but can I ask you something?'

Nagare turned. 'Certainly.'

'I heard you used to be a police detective. How on earth did you learn to cook like this?'

'Who told you I was with the police?'

'The editor of that magazine mentioned it.'

Nagare gave a dry chuckle. 'Ah. So Akane's been gossiping about me again.'

'Please don't take it the wrong way. I just couldn't help thinking . . . For a former detective to be making food of this quality must have required some pretty intensive training.'

'Oh, I don't think you could call it training. If I like something, I try making it. That's all.'

'Now you're just being modest.'

'No, I'm serious . . . Anyway, what makes you so curious?'

'Well, back where I'm from, I run this little business hotel. At the moment all we provide is a simple breakfast, but I'd like to serve proper meals one day. And if even an ex-detective – sorry, but you know what I mean – can get this good with a bit of training, I was thinking maybe I could, too.'

'Listen, it's like with anything in life: passion breeds proficiency. If you like cooking, all you have to do is stick at it long enough, and eventually you'll end up with something you're happy serving people.'

'If I like it, eh . . . See, that's the problem. I've never been very good at deciding what it is I actually *like*.' Shuji's gaze had drifted off into space.

'Guess you must have been blessed with plenty of choices along the way, then. Now, Koishi's ready to interview you, so just let me know when you're done here.' Nagare turned and made for the kitchen.

Still pondering his words, Shuji sat there silently eating the mushi-zushi, which had finally begun to cool.

Would the mushi-zushi in Onomichi have tasted like this?

He tried to remember what had made him so stubborn that day, but the answer eluded him. It was quite possible that he'd just been arguing for the sake of it.

He polished off every last grain of rice in the bowl. Nagare must have heard him setting his chopsticks down, because he promptly returned.

'Right. Shall I show you through?'

'Please.'

Shuji pushed himself up from the table, then followed Nagare down a narrow hallway.

'What are all these?' he asked, stopping to gaze at the photos that adorned practically every inch of the walls.

'Dishes I've made over the years. Just a way for me to keep track, really.' Nagare carried on walking. Shuji followed, his eyes still taking in the marvels on either side.

The building turned out to be much deeper than it was wide. In the room at the end of the hallway, which looked onto a small garden, he found Koishi waiting. She had changed into a black trouser suit.

'If you could just fill this out for me, please.'

Shuji smiled as he glanced over the form she had handed him on a clipboard. 'Reminds me of the register we have guests fill out at my hotel.'

He completed the sections for address, name, age and date of birth in no time at all, but paused when he came to the 'family details' section.

Koishi seemed to notice. 'Feel free to skip anything that's hard to fill out.'

'It's not exactly that it's hard . . .' murmured Shuji, half to himself. He completed and returned the form, then cleared his throat.

'Now then, Mr Shuji Kosaka, what dish are you looking for?' Koishi opened her notebook and gripped her pen.

'Gyoza dumplings.'

'What kind of gyoza are we talking?'

'Just . . . regular gyoza.'

'Right,' replied Koishi, before adding in an undertone: 'Very helpful . . .'

'Sorry.' Shuji gave an apologetic shrug. 'They really were just ordinary gyoza. Maybe a little spicier than usual, and the filling tasted sort of crispy. But that's about it.'

'No need to apologize. It's our job to find them, after all. Now, when and where did you eat these gyoza?'

'I was in my early twenties, which makes it more than fifteen years ago. I ate them at a ryokan in Utsukushigahara Onsen, over in Nagano prefecture.'

Koishi's eyes widened. 'They served *gyoza*? At a *ryokan*?'

'Not exactly.' Shuji sat up and leaned forward slightly. 'I guess I should start from the beginning.'

'Of course.'

'I went to university in Osaka. Tourism studies – you know, so I could take over the family business. There was a young woman in one of my classes whose family ran a ryokan in Nagano, and before I knew it we'd become an item.'

Koishi scribbled away wordlessly. Shuji paused, then went on.

'We started seeing each other not long after starting university. The thing is, there was another woman waiting for me back in Toyooka. A childhood friend I'd promised to marry.'

Koishi's expression stiffened noticeably. '. . . You were two-timing, in other words.'

'I never meant for things to end up that way, but yes – that's what it was.'

'Were you in love with them both?'

'I'm not sure if that's the right word. With Misako, who I'd known since I was a child, it was more like we'd always assumed we'd get married one day. I think our feelings for each other were a little different from most people's idea of romantic love.'

'Whereas the woman from Nagano – that was a more passionate affair, was it?'

'You could say that,' Shuji replied breezily.

'And you kept that up for the whole four years you were at university?'

'I did. I saw Yuri – that was her name, Yuri Inada – almost every day. We were what you'd call lovers. When she went back to Nagano in the summer and winter vacation, I went with her, staying at the family ryokan. I went back to Toyooka several times a year, too, and of course then I'd meet up with Misako and we'd talk about the future and things.'

'The dictionary definition of two-timing!' exclaimed Koishi, nostrils flaring. 'Sorry, but as a woman, I have to tell you this: you were way out of line.'

'I was, wasn't I? I knew I had to tell Yuri about Misako, but I could never seem to get the words out. In the meantime, her parents seemed to have assumed that Yuri and I were going to get married.'

Though he paused to let out the occasional sigh, there was something about Shuji's casual manner in relaying all this that was beginning to get on Koishi's nerves.

'What a horrible thing to do.'

'I know, I know. But I was just sort of going with the flow.'

'You were sitting on the fence is what you were doing,' Koishi snapped back.

'At the end of our last class together, right before we graduated, I finally managed to tell her about Misako. When I explained that I was already engaged to someone else, well . . .'

'What did she say?' asked Koishi, leaning forward.

'She didn't *say* anything. She walked off, and went straight back to her family home that very day.'

'I don't blame her. I'd have done the same – wait, no. I'd have slapped you a few times first.'

'Yuri was kind like that.'

'Yeah, and you took *advantage* of that kindness in order to—' Koishi stopped herself, then bowed slightly. 'Sorry, I'm getting carried away.'

'She disappeared completely after that. Didn't even come to our graduation ceremony. I decided I should apologize to her parents. After the ceremony I rushed straight to Nagano.'

'Bet they were furious.'

'The thing is, they weren't. Yuri hadn't told them. Turned out she'd gone travelling in Europe without explaining why. Still, all I could do was apologize. I explained the situation, then just kept saying sorry . . . I felt absolutely wretched. I mean, they'd always treated me like their own child.' Shuji's shoulders slumped as he went on. 'I'd been half expecting her father to punch me there and then, but they were just so understanding about it all – which only made it harder to bear . . .'

'They sound like good people.'

'I stayed late, thinking there was a chance Yuri might come home, and before I knew it I'd missed the last train. They put me up at the ryokan that night.'

'Now, that really is taking the—' Koishi put a hand to her mouth to stop herself.

'I know. Anyway, the meal they served me for lunch the next day was gyoza. That's what I was hoping you could recreate for me.'

'So that's where the gyoza come in.'

'I remember being a little surprised. They'd always cooked up all sorts of things whenever I stayed, but never gyoza.'

'Were they a favourite of Yuri's or something?'

'The opposite. We'd eaten together countless times in those four years, but I'd never seen her go near them. Even when I ordered some for us at a ramen place, she wouldn't touch them. I assumed she didn't like them.'

'Nagano . . . and gyoza,' said Koishi, sketching one of the dumplings. 'I wonder if there's some sort of connection.'

'Her father just kept telling me not to worry about it. Over and over. Her mother told me that Yuri would get over it. That I should just try to be happy.' By now, an unmistakeable sheen had formed in Shuji's eyes.

'Sounds like you got lucky,' murmured Koishi, her nose flushed red with emotion.

Shuji dropped his gaze. 'It was a tough time.'

'But . . . why go looking for these gyoza again now?'

'Lately I've been feeling a little . . . tired of it all. At home, I sometimes feel like I can hardly breathe.'

'Not getting on so well with your wife, then?'

'Well, we've known each other for over three decades. Hardly surprising if we're a little . . . fed up with each other, is it?'

'*Fed up* with each other?' Koishi repeated with a grimace.

Shuji smiled faintly. 'You'll understand when you get married, I'm sure.'

'I don't think I want to,' replied Koishi, puffing out her cheeks.

'Anyway,' said Shuji, a pensive look coming into his eyes, 'with life dragging on and on, it suddenly came back to me the other day. The gyoza I ate at that ryokan.'

Koishi narrowed her eyes at him. 'I hope you're not about to tell me you're thinking about getting back together with Yuri.'

'Of course not. I'm sure she's forgotten all about me by now.'

'Women don't forget. Not when they loved someone from the bottom of their heart.'

'Is that so . . .'

At the sight of the tears in his eyes, Koishi felt something bitter welling up inside her. 'Well, what are you hoping to achieve by eating the gyoza, then?'

'Oh, nothing in particular,' said Shuji, averting his eyes to escape her glare. 'I just want to eat them, that's all.'

'Right. Then I guess we'll find them.'

Koishi gave a deep sigh, then closed her notebook with a swift, almost violent motion.

'All okay?' asked Nagare, getting up from the counter where he'd been sitting.

Shuji stopped and bowed. 'We had a good long chat.'

'I almost forgot,' said Koishi, reopening her notebook on the counter. 'What was the name of the ryokan where you ate the gyoza?'

'The Inada Ryokan, in the Utsukushigahara Onsen area.'

'And it's still in business?'

Shuji cocked his head. 'I'm . . . not sure. I haven't been in touch with them since.'

'A ryokan that serves . . . gyoza?' asked Nagare, glancing at the pair in confusion.

'I'll explain later, Dad,' said Koishi. He responded with a slight nod.

'When do you think you might manage it by?' asked Shuji.

'How about you come back in two weeks?' replied Nagare. 'That's if I've cracked it, of course.'

'Got it. I'll be looking forward to it.'

'We'll contact you on your mobile, if that's okay?' asked Koishi, before asking for his number.

'Oh,' said Shuji, unzipping the bag at his waist, 'can I pay for the meal?'

'You can pay for it all at the end.'

Shuji nodded and zipped the bag up once more.

After seeing Shuji off, the pair sat down at one of the tables.

'What's all this about gyoza at a ryokan, then?' asked Nagare. 'Wait, let me guess: it's complicated.'

'You could say that.' Koishi opened her notebook on the table. 'But as long as you can speak to the ryokan's owners, this one should be a breeze.'

'Since when has this job ever been a "breeze"? Anyway, if it were that simple, he wouldn't have come all this way to ask for our help.' Nagare made a sour face as he flicked through Koishi's notes.

'I guess you're right . . .' replied Koishi sullenly as she made them a pot of tea.

'What's got into you, then?'

'I just got so angry while I was listening to him, Dad. I know, I know, this is our job. But he really rubbed me up the wrong way.' Koishi poured the tea so forcefully that it spilled over the sides of the cup.

'No need to take it out on the tea. Anyway, like you said, it's our job.'

'I know, but the idea of helping that spineless good-for-nothing . . .'

'Watch that tongue of yours, Koishi. What am I always telling you? We're not here to judge the client. We're here to find their food.'

Koishi fell silent, though her lips still quivered with anger.

'Anyway,' he went on, 'looks like I'm off to Nagano. Fancy tagging along? I know a good soba place.'

'No chance.' Koishi turned aside in exasperation. 'You're on your own with this one, Dad.'

2

It had only been three weeks, but the sunlight in Kyoto had grown noticeably warmer. In fact, the breeze that buffeted Shuji's cheeks as he made the now-familiar journey along Shomen-dori was positively springlike.

He stopped in front of the Kamogawa Diner, crouching to pet a tabby cat he found sprawled by the entrance.

'Where did *you* come from, then?'

Without changing position in the slightest, the cat closed its eyes and mewed softly.

'Technically, he's ours,' said Koishi, looking down at Shuji from the doorway. 'Not that Dad ever lets him in.'

'Is that so? He seems half-asleep.'

'That's his default setting. It's why we named him Drowsy.'

'Well then, Drowsy, guess I'll see you later.' Shuji got to his feet and brushed his hands off.

'Sorry it took a little longer than expected,' called Nagare from inside.

'Not at all,' replied Shuji as he walked in and removed his white, slightly cropped jacket. 'It's not like I'm in a rush. Plus the timing meant I got to see the plum trees while they're in bloom.'

Koishi looked up from the table she'd begun wiping. 'You've been sightseeing?'

'The Kitano Tenmangu Shrine,' said Shuji, unslinging his waist bag as he sat down. 'I visited the plum orchard before coming here. Can almost still smell them . . .'

'Well, I think I've figured out these gyoza of yours. I'll fry them up now – just give me a moment.' Nagare made his way into the kitchen.

'Normally only takes him two weeks,' explained Koishi. 'But this one took a little extra effort. He ended up going to Nagano *twice*.' Her tone of voice made it clear that she wanted Shuji to know they had done him a very big favour.

He lowered his head in apology. 'Sorry to put him to so much trouble.'

Koishi snorted. 'Don't worry. He likes the tough ones.'

'That does make me feel a little better.'

'What'll you be drinking? Beer?'

'No, I want to be able to taste the gyoza properly. Just tea will be fine.'

'Alright then. I'll brew you some.'

Koishi set a white place mat down on the laminated table, then headed for the kitchen. From it came the sound of something sizzling in a pan – accompanied by an enticing fragrance. The gyoza were on their way, then. Shuji's chest tightened with anticipation.

'Here we go,' said Nagare when he returned. 'I believe this was how they served them.' He set a round, Western-style plate, its rim decorated with red floral patterns, down on the place mat.

'That's right. They looked just like this.' Shuji leaned forward and took a deep sniff. 'Smelled the same too, I think.'

'And the dipping sauce wasn't in one of the usual little dishes, was it? It was in a bowl.'

'That's right. We all sat around the table, each dipping our gyoza in a bowl just like this.'

'Of course, the plate would have been bigger, with more gyoza on it. It's just you today, so I've scaled it down.'

Twenty or so of the dumplings had been piled seemingly at random on the old-fashioned plate, clumped together in groups of four or five. It was all exactly as Shuji remembered.

'Well, enjoy!'

As Nagare retreated from the table, Koishi stepped forward with an earthenware Arita pot and accompanying cup, which she left on the table.

At first, Shuji simply sat there, motionless, gazing at the gyoza. By the time he roused himself and reached for his chopsticks, the dumplings had cooled considerably.

He lowered one into the bowl of dipping sauce – a combination of soy sauce and vinegar – then brought it to his mouth.

The soft, springy texture. The golden, perfectly cooked skin. The crispy, crunchy filling. Everything about the gyoza was, as far as he could tell, identical to the ones he'd eaten all those years ago.

Shuji carried on munching away at the gyoza, noticing how the initial sharpness of the flavour slowly gave way to a pleasant, slightly bitter tang. If his admittedly hazy memories were correct, the same had been true of the gyoza at the ryokan.

'Did I get it right?' said Nagare, who had arrived at his side.

'Yes. I mean, it was such a long time ago that I can't be exactly sure. But something tells me this was how they tasted.'

'Glad to hear it.' Nagare smiled with relief. 'I sampled a few of them while I was making them – they are good, aren't they?'

'Sorry,' said Shuji, bowing slightly in his seat. 'Sounds like I sent you on a bit of a wild goose chase.'

'All in a day's work.'

Shuji dabbed at his mouth with a handkerchief. 'How *did* you manage it?'

'Mind if I take a seat?'

'Please.'

Nagare sat down opposite him. 'I suspect you already know that the Inada Ryokan is no longer in business. When you visited us last time, you said you weren't sure – but then there is such a thing as the internet these days. It wouldn't exactly be hard for you to find out.'

Shuji smiled faintly. 'I'm sorry. I did know. I was worried that if I told you, you might turn me down on account of it being too difficult.'

'Never mind that. Anyway, all I could do was ask around. I talked to the owners of every ryokan in the area, and they all remembered the Inadas. Told me all sorts about them. Only problem was, no one knew anything about any gyoza.'

'I'm not surprised. I mean, I can't imagine they ever served them to guests.'

'After coming back to Kyoto empty-handed, I decided to make another visit. At first that didn't go too well either. I was about ready to give up and head home when I spotted an old, rustic-looking ryokan I hadn't been to yet. Thought

I might as well poke my head inside. Well, what do you know: it turned out one of their staff used to be the doorman at the Inada Ryokan.'

'The doorman? Not . . . Mr Sugi?'

'Well remembered! That's the man. Works as a receptionist for the Hanaoka Ryokan these days. He was the one who told me about these gyoza.'

Shuji smiled. 'Was he well?'

'He's almost eighty-five.' Nagare produced a photo and laid it on the table. 'Legs aren't in great shape, so he can't move about too much, but he does a fine job of manning that reception desk. He's become the face of the Hanaoka Ryokan.'

Shuji picked the photo up and gazed at it for some time. 'He hasn't changed all that much, you know.'

'Turns out the Inadas were old friends of the Hanaokas, so after their ryokan closed, quite a few of their staff moved over to the Hanaoka Ryokan. By now, of course, they've all retired – apart from Mr Sugi, that is.'

'Is that so . . .' Shuji glanced up at Nagare. 'And the Inadas? Are they . . .'

'Both passed away, I'm afraid. Not long after closing down their ryokan.'

Shuji nodded silently in response.

'Now, about these gyoza . . .'

'Come to think of it, I remember Mr Sugi eating them

with us,' said Shuji. He was still holding the photo, though his gaze had drifted up towards the ceiling.

'It turns out they were one of the most popular dishes at the Inada Ryokan.'

Shuji blinked in surprise. 'They . . . were?'

'Not among the guests, mind you. Among the staff. Out of all the food the Inadas provided, these gyoza were by far their favourite.'

'I can see why. I mean, they're pretty special.'

'Now, the turnover among ryokan staff can be pretty high. Lots of them quit after just a short spell on the job.'

'It's the same at our hotel,' Shuji put in. 'The work's so tough a lot of people can't hack it.'

'Well, whenever someone left, the Inadas would always serve them these gyoza on their last day. As a sort of parting gift – a final memory to take with them.'

Shuji stared down at the plate of gyoza in silence.

'Azumino, just north of Utsukushigahara Onsen, is famous for its wasabi,' continued Nagare. 'The Inadas added it to their gyoza. They'd pickle the stems and leaves in brine, then chop them up and add them to the filling.'

'So *that's* what that flavour is. Sort of sharp and bitter.'

'Pickled wasabi doesn't have the "kick" you get from the raw stuff, but it still gives the flavours a real boost. Adds a nice crunch, too.'

'I had no idea they'd put so much thought into them.'

Shuji slipped one of the remaining – and now almost cold – gyoza into his mouth.

'Brought you a fresh pot of tea,' said Koishi, arriving with a Mashiko-ware teapot.

'Mr Sugi told me that when you work in a ryokan, the staff become a sort of second family,' continued Nagare.

'They say that at my hotel, too,' said Shuji, putting his chopsticks down. 'Comes from spending so much time in each other's company, I guess.'

'Anyway, over time, these gyoza came to symbolize the sadness of saying goodbye,' said Nagare, gazing down at the dumplings still on the plate. 'In fact, the staff started referring to them as the "farewell special".'

Shuji had been about to take a sip of his tea, but now his eyes rose to meet Nagare's. 'The . . . farewell special, eh?'

'I had a wife too, you know. Kikuko. Unlike you, I was never much of a ladies' man. For me, it was Kikuko all the way. But when she passed away, I couldn't be there at her side. That's not something you get over fast. I mean, all those years together, and I didn't even manage to see her off properly . . .'

Shuji seemed uncertain where the conversation was going. But Koishi was nodding deeply.

'Towards the end, I kept telling her we should phone Dad,' she explained. 'Tell him she might not have long left. But even when she was starting to fade, she kept snapping at me, saying we shouldn't distract Dad from his work. And then . . . that was it. She was gone.'

'Marrying someone is a funny thing,' continued Nagare. 'You're not even joined by blood, and yet you end up understanding each other better than anyone. Which means there's no hiding anything.'

Koishi was nodding vigorously again, though Shuji remained silent.

'Sure there's nothing else you'd like to ask?' she said.

But Nagare rose from his seat as if to cut her off. 'He's told us plenty already. Said all he needs to say.' He glanced at Shuji. 'Isn't that right?'

'It is,' said Shuji, getting to his feet and bowing to them. 'Thank you very much.'

'You're welcome,' said Nagare, holding his gaze.

Koishi seemed unconvinced. 'You're . . . sure that's everything?'

'Yes,' replied Shuji, somewhat forcefully. 'I'm fine.'

'You know, I have plenty of regrets myself,' said Nagare. 'Should have done this and not that. Should have chosen that path instead of this one. But the sad truth is there's no going back.'

'Thank you for everything you've done. Now, how much do I owe you?' Shuji produced a wallet from his waist bag.

'However much you feel it was worth. Just send it to this account,' said Koishi, handing him a slip of paper.

'I'll do that right away.' Shuji tucked his wallet back into the bag, then reached for his white jacket.

'Looks like you brought us a souvenir,' said Nagare, plucking a plum petal from the jacket's shoulder.

'Oh,' said Shuji, staring at the petal in Nagare's hand. 'Must have fallen on me at the shrine.'

'How does that tanka poem go again?' said Koishi. Then she recited:

> *When the east wind blows,*
> *Let it send your fragrance,*
> *Oh plum blossoms.*
> *Although your master is gone,*
> *Do not forget the spring.*

'. . . Something like that, anyway.'

Nagare nodded. 'Love is a force to be reckoned with. But it can also be a pretty short-lived affair.' He blew into his hand, and the petal went fluttering into the air.

'Ah, Drowsy,' said Shuji, leaning down to rub the cat's chin. 'I'll be back soon, don't worry.'

'Is it still cold in Toyooka?' asked Koishi, squatting at his side.

'Colder than here, yes. But spring's just about starting to show.'

'Here's the recipe for those gyoza,' said Nagare, handing him an envelope. 'Just in case.'

'Thank you,' replied Shuji with a pained grin. 'Don't think I'll be making them, though.'

'You take care of yourself, you hear?'

'You too. And . . . thank you both very much.'

Shuji gave a quick bow, bid them farewell, and turned west. As his figure receded down Shomen-dori, Drowsy mewed a quiet goodbye of his own.

'Well, that's a relief,' said Koishi once Shuji had disappeared from view.

'What is?' replied Nagare.

'Isn't it obvious? He's finally given up on Yuri. From now on it's going to be all about his wife.'

'Oh, I don't know about that. Apparently Yuri's still single.'

'Really? But then . . . why did you bring Mum up like that?'

'Listen, my job is finding people's food. What they do next is none of my business.' Nagare made his way back inside, followed by Koishi. 'Now, what do you say we invite Hiroshi over this evening? Have ourselves a little gyoza party.'

'Really?' All of a sudden, Koishi's eyes were sparkling.

'They always taste better when there's a crowd.'

'Wait,' said Koishi, her expression freezing. 'This isn't because Hiroshi has made some sort of . . . decision, is it?'

'Oh, no. We don't do "farewell gyoza" at the Kamogawa Diner.' Nagare kneeled by the family altar and lit a stick of incense. 'Do we, Kikuko?'

'Phew!' Koishi patted her father on the back. 'How about "happily ever after" gyoza instead?'

Nagare pulled a face, then joined his hands together in prayer.

'Hear that, Kikuko? Send a little happiness her way, would you?'

Chapter 5:

Omurice

1

Moments after arriving at Kyoto station, Takayuki Jojima hurried out of the Hachijo exit, towards the taxi rank and into one of the waiting vehicles.

'This street, please,' he said, holding out a map.

'Ah,' replied the driver once he'd donned his reading glasses. 'Shomen-dori. One of the altar shops?'

'No. The Kamogawa Diner.'

'Hmm. Can't say I remember anything like that around there . . .' The driver removed his glasses and returned his hands to the wheel. 'Well, let's see what we find, eh?'

As they drove up onto the bridge that would bring them round to the north side of the station, the phrase 'purple hills and crystal waters', an old poetic shorthand for Kyoto's scenic beauty, came to Takayuki's mind. The hilly Higashiyama area to the east was veiled in a purplish spring haze, and chances were good that the waters of the Kamogawa were looking pretty crystalline, too.

Good old Rai San'yo, he thought, recalling the poet who'd coined the phrase. *Not that he came up in our exam in the end.* Takayuki was thinking of the university entrance examination he'd taken some twenty-five years previously.

The black taxi passed over the railway lines before heading towards Kyoto Tower and then north on Karasuma-dori. Just before Higashi Honganji temple, the driver flicked his right indicator on, turned onto a side street and glanced at Takayuki.

'We'll have to go round this way. Shomen-dori is one-way.'

Two left turns later, they were cruising slowly down the street in question.

'I think this is it.'

The driver applied the brakes with a dubious expression. 'Doesn't look like a restaurant to me.'

'No, this is the place.' Takayuki handed him a thousand-yen note. 'I heard it doesn't exactly look the part.'

A weathered two-storey building. Walls of faded grey mortar. No sign, or anything else indicating the presence of a restaurant. In other words, everything he'd been told to expect. Takayuki removed his grey coat and slid the door open.

'Hello?' came the voice of Koishi Kamogawa, clad in a black sommelier's apron.

'Is this the Kamogawa Diner?'

'That's right. Here for a meal?'

'Actually, I'd like you to track one down for me.'

'Ah, so you're a *client*, then. You saw our advert?'

'Advert? What advert?'

'You . . . didn't read about us in *Gourmet Monthly*?'

'No. Hisahiko told me about you.'

'Hisahiko?'

'Ah,' said Nagare, arriving in his chef's whites. 'You mean Hisahiko Tsuda, if I'm not mistaken? Been spreading the word, has he?'

'That's right.' Their new client held out a business card. 'My name is Takayuki Jojima.'

'Nagare Kamogawa. And this is my daughter, Koishi, who runs the detective agency.'

Koishi nodded politely, then gave Takayuki a puzzled look. 'Wait . . . do you mean Mr Tsuda as in . . . Tsuda Enterprises?'

'That's the one. He's CEO of the group I work for. Younger than me, actually, which is why he insists on me calling him by his first name. I know it's odd to refer to my boss like that, but he's always been Hisahiko to me.'

'Is he well, then?' asked Koishi.

'Oh, yes. Firing on all cylinders.' Takayuki gave a slightly ironic smile.

'Glad to hear it,' said Nagare.

'He asked me to tell you that he's helped his stepmother move to Tokyo, and she lives with him now.'

Takayuki produced a photo from his briefcase and handed it to Nagare. It had been taken on the large square in front of the Imperial Palace in Tokyo, and showed Hisahiko Tsuda standing next to his wheelchair-bound stepmother. They were both grinning broadly at the camera.

Nagare smiled as he handed back the photo. 'Wonderful to hear.'

'He told me you cook up a storm . . .'

'I ask first-time customers to leave the menu up to me. That alright with you?'

'Of course.'

'Then just give me a moment.' Nagare bustled off towards the kitchen, adjusting his chef's hat.

'I'm *very* excited about this,' said Takayuki as he hung his coat on a nearby rack.

Koishi glanced at his business card as she poured him some tea. 'Managing Director, Tsuda Food Services. So do you . . . run restaurants or something?'

'Izakaya-style places, mainly.' Takayuki took a sip of the tea. 'Heard of Idaten? It's a chain.'

'Oh, I've been to one of those! Food's great – easy on

the wallet, too. So Mr Tsuda owns those too, does he? I had no idea . . . Now, what'd you like to drink with your meal?'

'Mind if I take a look at the food before I decide?'

'Of course. Can't offer you anything *too* fancy, but Dad and I both like a drink, so there's a decent selection. Just let me know when you're ready to order something.'

'Thanks. Pretty partial to a tipple myself.'

'Sorry to keep you waiting.' Nagare had arrived with a large, lidded bamboo basket on a silver tray. 'Bit early for cherry-blossom viewing, but I've put together a picnic-style spread.' He set the basket down in front of Takayuki and removed the lid.

'Wow . . . Isn't that something!' Takayuki's eyes were two round orbs of excitement.

'Let me take you through it. The skewers in the top left are inspired by those coloured mochi balls people like to eat at this time of year. Shrimp dumplings, baby cucumber and quail meatballs, all speared onto a willow branch. The thick omelette next to that is the sort of tamagoyaki you'd get at a Tokyo sushi restaurant – cooked with shrimp paste. Then you have the sawara mackerel, grilled Kyoto-style in a sweet white miso marinade, and in the small bowl below, a selection of steamed vegetables. Baby taro, Kintoki carrot, pumpkin, lotus root and Shogoin turnip. On that tissue paper in the middle are various edible wild plants, all deep-fried: ostrich fern, butterbur buds, momiji-gasa, angelica buds and mugwort. Those are good with a bit of matcha salt, or you might want to try dipping them in the Worcestershire-style sauce in that little pot. To the left of that, wrapped in the green bamboo leaf, is cherry bass sushi, while the small bowl next to that is flash-boiled Omi beef, with a ponzu vinegar gelée. I'll bring the rice and soup through shortly – in the meantime, enjoy. Oh, and how about that drink?'

'I mean, with a spread like this, how can I say no? I think it has to be sake.'

'Want me to warm it up for you? It's that in-between season where it's hard to decide, isn't it . . .'

'Room temperature is fine, thanks. I'll leave the brand up to you.'

'Sounds good. I'll bring a few bottles through for you to choose from.' Nagare hurried off to the kitchen.

'You like your sake, then?' asked Koishi. 'In my experience it's only the seasoned drinkers who like it at room temperature. My grandfather, for one . . .'

Takayuki gave a cheerful shrug. 'Guilty as charged. Once I start I can't stop.'

Nagare reappeared cradling four large bottles of sake, which he set down on the table. 'This is Suigei, brewed in Kochi. The Sasanokawa is from Fukushima, then you have Denshu from Aomori, and Isojiman from Shizuoka. All of the junmai type. I do have some Kyoto sakes too, but these would be my picks if you're drinking at room temperature.'

Takayuki folded his arms, an impressed look on his face. 'Well, you obviously know how to pick your sake. Almost makes me want to try all of them.'

'Well, in that case, I'll leave them all out. Feel free to mix and match.' Nagare set a selection of large sake cups down alongside the bamboo basket. Takayuki wasted no time in pouring some of the Isojiman into one of them.

'Now I see what Hisahiko meant when he said this place was something else. It was worth coming here for this meal alone.'

'Well, I hope it's all to your liking.' Nagare withdrew to the kitchen, followed by Koishi.

At first, Takayuki simply sat there, gazing at the basket so intently that you might have thought he was trying to bore a hole into it. *Now I know what people mean when they talk about 'feasting your eyes' on something*, he thought as he licked his lips.

He drained his first cup of sake, then manoeuvred his chopsticks towards their first destination: the thick shrimp-paste omelette. Layered and rolled into a fragrant, cake-like sponge, it was an irresistible combination of savoury and sweet – just the way Takayuki liked it.

Next, he began loosening the various elements from the willow skewer and popping them into his mouth. The shrimp dumplings were succulent, the salted cucumber refreshing, and the quail meatballs – which included the soft bones ground up in the paste – dense with rich flavour.

Takayuki reached for an Iga-ware sake cup and filled it to the brim with the Sasanokawa. Then he sprinkled some of the matcha salt on one of the deep-fried butterbur buds and slipped it into his mouth. He crunched away, savouring the flavour, then gulped down the sake. He reached for one of the angelica buds, dunked it in the Worcestershire-style sauce, then chewed thoughtfully on it. After a moment's hesitation, he poured himself a cup of the Suigei, then drank the whole thing in one go.

Getting himself tipsy as soon as possible – when it came to drinking, that had always been Takayuki's priority.

'How's everything, then?' asked Nagare, arriving behind him.

'Hisahiko set my expectations pretty high, but you've blown them out of the water. It's so delicious that I've been enjoying this sake at quite a lick.'

'Yes – you can handle your drink, I see!' said Nagare, eyeing the bottles at his side.

Takayuki hunched his shoulders apologetically. 'Not the most refined habit, I know.'

'Just let me know when you'd like that rice.'

After Nagare had returned to the kitchen, he turned his attention to the Kyoto-style grilled sawara and the steamed vegetables. By now, he'd consumed at least half a litre of sake, but he was yet to feel its effects. With a resigned sigh, he called out for the rice.

'I hope I'm not rushing you,' said Nagare as he arrived.

'Not at all. If I sip away like this all day, I'll be in no state to explain what it is I'm looking for.'

'Today's rice is with bamboo shoots. They're an early harvest from Tokushima – marinated in a sansho-pepper-infused soy sauce, charcoal-grilled, chopped up and steamed with the rice. You might want to add a sprinkle of these chopped sansho leaves, too. The soup is a salty sea bream broth, with freshly harvested wakame seaweed.'

Nagare removed the lid from the Oribe clay pot, letting out a rush of steam. A delectable fragrance swept across the table.

'I'll definitely add the sansho leaves. I've always had a soft spot for sharp, herbal flavours.'

'Good to hear. Well, enjoy!'

Nagare set a rice paddle and Kyo-ware bowl down on the table together with a lidded soup bowl, then left him alone once more. Takayuki leaned towards the column of steam issuing from the clay pot and closed his eyes in bliss.

Living on his own as he did, this sort of rice – with extra ingredients steamed in the same pot – was not something he often found himself eating. He filled the bowl, scattered over plenty of the sansho leaves and, before he knew it, had devoured the lot.

From the black lacquered soup bowl, meanwhile, came a refined, briny aroma. There was an expression, *sankai no chinmi*, that meant 'delicacies from both land and sea' and referred to an extravagant spread of food. Right now, Takayuki couldn't shake it from his mind.

By the time he'd refilled and depleted his rice bowl twice, he was finally starting to feel full. Slowly massaging his belly, Takayuki set down his chopsticks, a look of utter contentment on his face.

'Brought you some iribancha tea,' said Nagare, placing a Seto-ware teapot on the table and lifting its lid. 'Quite a sharp aroma on it – hope you don't mind?'

Takayuki sniffed the pot, nostrils twitching, then nodded deeply. 'Not at all.'

'Nice after a meal, I find,' said Nagare, pouring the tea into a tall cup. 'Good for the digestion – and clears the mind.'

Takayuki took a sip, then peered over at the kitchen. 'Your daughter must be waiting.'

'She's in the office at the back. I'll show you through when you're ready.'

'I'm all set.' Takayuki put his glasses on and got to his feet.

'Interesting layout,' said Takayuki as Nagare guided him down a long hallway. 'I see what people mean about Kyoto houses being like eel beds.'

'Yes. Narrow at the front, but it runs pretty far back. Most old houses around here are built this way.'

'And the photos? Did you make all these dishes?'

Nagare turned and smiled. 'I did. These walls are a diary of sorts. It's not all food, either – there are a few other memories mixed in there, too.'

Takayuki stopped and began gazing with admiration at the photos. 'I can see lots of Western food here. Chinese, too . . . oh, and that looks Korean? Real jack of all trades, aren't you?'

'And master of none,' replied Nagare without stopping. 'Never quite got around to specializing in any one cuisine, see.'

'That's probably a good thing. Much better than spending your whole life trying to perfect a single dish.'

'I don't know about that. Anyway, I'll leave you with Koishi.' Nagare opened the door at the end of the corridor, then made his way back to the restaurant.

'No need to sit on the edge like that,' said Koishi as Takayuki attempted to perch on one end of the sofa. 'Try the middle?'

'Sorry. Feeling a little nervous, is all.'

Koishi grinned. 'Don't worry. I'm not going to grill you.'

'I have . . . bad memories of these sorts of situations,' said Takayuki, slowly shuffling towards the middle of the sofa.

'Could you start by filling this out? Just roughly is fine.'

'Certainly.' Takayuki began jotting down his details on the form she'd handed him.

'Takayuki Jojima,' read Koishi once he'd returned it to her. 'Forty-three. From Karatsu, Saga. Whereabouts is that again?'

'Down in Kyushu. Just west of Fukuoka.'

'And now you live in Koganei. No family to speak of?'

'Nope. I'm a lone wolf . . . Sorry, that's quite a dramatic way of putting it.'

'Married?'

'Twice – and divorced twice. Right away, in both cases.'

'Any children?'

'Never got round to it.'

'Oh dear. You must get a little lonely sometimes.'

'Makes life a lot simpler, to be honest. Do you have a partner yourself?'

Koishi made a wry face. 'I haven't exactly come across many suitable candidates.'

'Well, when one does come along, I'm sure you'll have no trouble winning him over.'

'Appreciate the vote of confidence. Now, what's this dish you're looking for?'

'Omurice.'

Koishi couldn't help but chuckle. 'Omelette on fried rice? Every little boy's favourite.'

'Not quite what you expected from someone my age, then?'

'No, but there's nothing wrong with that. Did you eat it when you were young?'

'I was in my final year of high school. So . . . twenty-five years ago.'

'And was this at home? Or a restaurant?'

Takayuki let out a quiet sigh. 'Actually, my friend's mother cooked it for me.'

'Right. Did you go to school in Saga, then?'

'I did.'

'And your friend's mother – is she still around?'

'I believe so, yes.'

'Then . . . couldn't you just ask her for the recipe?'

'Well,' frowned Takayuki, 'actually, I came here because that's precisely what I *don't* want to do.'

'Of course. Sorry.' Koishi opened her notebook. 'Well, tell me all about it.'

'See, you might not be able to tell now, but I was a pretty bright kid.'

'Oh, I definitely took you for the brainy type.'

'I had my sights set on the national university in Fukuoka. My teacher said I was practically guaranteed to pass the entrance exams.'

'So you really were bright, then.'

'In the spring of my third year of high school, my friend – Shinji Kawanami, his name is – told me his mother wanted me to become his home tutor.'

'But you were in the same year, weren't you?'

'Yes, that's why I refused at first. But Asako – that's his mother – was really persistent. In the end I agreed to help Shinji out once a week.'

'So it was Asako Kawanami who cooked the omurice, then.' Koishi's pen was racing across her notebook.

'She was a very kind woman. I'd lost my mother as a child, see, but she cared for me like her own son.'

'Nothing like home cooking, is there? Even if it wasn't technically *your* home . . .'

'Exactly.' Takayuki closed his eyes. 'Everything she made was just so . . . delicious.'

'So every time you went over there to tutor Shinji, she'd cook something up for you?'

'Yes. I'd turn up at five o'clock on a Saturday evening, help Shinji for three hours, and then she'd serve us dinner before I went home.'

'If everything she made was delicious, then why the omurice in particular?'

'Well, it was my personal favourite.'

'Let me guess. You've tried all sorts of omurice since, but none of them have ever beaten Asako's. Is that right?'

'Not exactly. Actually, I've never eaten it again.'

Koishi looked up at him. 'Never? As in . . .'

'She made it for me on my last day as Shinji's tutor.' He pursed his lips. 'And since then, I've never eaten omurice again.'

'Not sure I follow,' said Koishi, knitting her brows.

Takayuki resettled himself on the sofa. 'Of course. I should probably explain, shouldn't I?'

'Please.' Koishi leaned forward, pen at the ready.

'On my first evening as tutor, she made us tonkatsu. The following week it was croquettes, and after that it was curry.' Takayuki tilted his head back and stared at the ceiling. 'They all tasted *incredible*.'

'I can tell. You even remember the exact dishes.'

'Well, it was the highlight of my week. I wasn't a huge eater myself, but Shinji had a real appetite on him, and he'd always ask for seconds. When Asako brought us home three bowls of eel rice from Takeya – that's a nearby restaurant that's famous for the dish – he even ended up eating some of hers.'

'Is Karatsu famous for eel, then?'

'Not particularly, but that Takeya place was really something. I'd cover mine with sansho pepper, but Shinji would just wolf it down as it was. Asako would sit there watching him with this dreamy look in her eyes.'

'Oh, I can just picture it,' said Koishi, by now scribbling away. 'Parents love to see their kids eating well.'

'I'm almost a year older than Shinji, but because my birthday's the fifth of April and his is the thirtieth of March, we ended up in the same grade at school. I think that's why he always seemed to look up to me. Even talked to me in this respectful sort of tone.'

'That's sweet. I always wished I had an older brother.'

'The evening she served us curry, Asako asked what my favourite dish was. I didn't have to think twice. My own mother passed away when I was eight, and I couldn't remember much of what she'd cooked me. The one dish that I *could* remember was omurice.'

'So Asako made it for you.'

'Yes – the very next Saturday. It tasted . . . heavenly, is the word that comes to mind. Asako was delighted when she saw how much I was enjoying it. After that, she made it every other time I went there, and sometimes two weeks in a row. I'd spend the whole week waiting for Saturday evening to roll around.'

'It was that good, was it?'

'The rice was stuffed with bits of fried chicken and onion. Not too sweet, but ever so fragrant, and it tasted . . . familiar, somehow. Meanwhile, the omelette covering the rice was cooked to perfection – and as for the tomato sauce she'd ladle on top, it was just . . . out of this world.' Takayuki was staring wistfully into the middle distance.

'The sauce wasn't just ketchup, then?'

'I think there might have been some in there, but it wasn't sweet like ketchup is. It tasted more . . . refined than that, somehow.'

'A refined tomato sauce,' said Koishi, noting this down. 'Any other distinctive features?'

'Hmm . . .' Takayuki crossed his arms. 'What else was there . . .'

'We'll probably need a little more to go on. Anything at all will help.'

'Well, I'm not sure if this is relevant, but . . . like I said, Shinji would normally gobble down anything you put in front of him. But when we had omurice, he'd never finish his meal.'

'He wasn't a fan of omurice, then?'

'No, that wasn't it. Whenever they served it at the school cafeteria, he always asked for an extra big portion.'

'Intriguing,' said Koishi, a puzzled look on her face.

'Whenever I asked him why he wouldn't finish it, he'd just fall silent. I don't know the reason to this day.'

'I still don't get why you haven't eaten it since.'

'Ah, yes. The most important part. Sorry, could I get some water?'

'Oh! Forgot to make you some tea, didn't I?'

Koishi scrabbled to her feet, filled a paper cup with water from the dispenser, then handed it to him. Takayuki downed it in one. When he continued, it was in a slightly strained voice.

'The long and short of it is, Shinji passed the entrance exam, and I didn't.'

'Wait, what?'

'I remember standing there in front of the board where they'd posted the results, unable to believe my eyes. I'd been so focused on helping Shinji pass that it never even crossed my mind that I might fail.'

'What . . . happened?'

Takayuki frowned. 'I don't know. Must have made some sort of horrible mistake somewhere. Without even realizing it.'

'Asako must have been pretty shocked too.'

'We'd all gone to check the results together. I could tell she found the whole situation unbearable. She ended up crying. Got down on her knees, begging me to forgive her. Somehow Shinji and I both ended up on the floor too, bawling our eyes out.'

'Sheesh, life really knows how to throw a curveball. What were the odds of that happening?'

'I only had my own incompetence to blame,' said

Takayuki, clenching his fists slightly. 'All I managed to say to Shinji was that I was glad he'd passed.'

There was a lengthy silence.

'Must have been a tough moment for both of you,' said Koishi eventually.

'Actually,' replied Takayuki, eyes downcast, 'I think it was Asako who took it hardest.'

'I can imagine. I mean, if you hadn't spent all those hours tutoring Shinji, the results might have been the other way round.'

'Maybe – or maybe I still would have messed up. Who's to say?'

'Right. So, after that, omurice wasn't exactly . . .'

'My life started to go off the rails. Nothing was working out the way I'd planned it. And I got it into my head that the omurice somehow marked the turning point.'

Koishi nodded, frowning.

'After that, I lost it slightly,' he went on. 'Started thinking my only purpose in life was to pit my own success against Shinji's. Waiting a year to resit the exam wasn't an option, so I ended up at a less prestigious university, but the company I eventually began working for – a major trading conglomerate – was a cut above the one *he* ended up at.'

Koishi couldn't help noticing the flash of pride in Takayuki's expression as he said these words.

'Your best friend became your rival, then.'

'When I heard he'd quit in order to found his own company, I did the same. When I heard he'd married a flight attendant, I married one from a rival airline.'

Koishi was dumbfounded. 'Wow. You really went all in.'

'The difference was that it was all plain sailing for Shinji, whereas everything I tried my hand at seemed to go wrong. Soon his company was taking the market by storm, while mine had flopped miserably. That was around the time my wife left me.'

Takayuki let out a long sigh. Koishi did the same. 'I . . . don't even know what to say.'

'His business grew like crazy. Now it's the parent company of the Kawanami Group. Fifty subsidiaries, last time I counted. And their main rival is Tsuda Enterprises.'

'Right. So *that's* how you ended up working for Mr Tsuda.'

'Yes.' Takayuki gave a self-deprecating snort. 'Though I'm small fry at the company, really.'

'The Kawanami Group . . . wait, do they own River Wave?'

'The diner chain? Yeah. Doing so well they've even opened up branches abroad. That's what they're most known for, but they do all sorts. Property, finance, you name it.'

'And this Shinji is *the* Shinji Kawanami? The one who's always on talk shows and in magazines and things? But he's *super* famous!'

'That's him. I turn the TV off whenever his face appears.' He gave another snort. 'Not a magazine person, so I wouldn't know about those.'

'Can I just check something?' Koishi gripped her pen once more.

'Go ahead,' replied Takayuki, returning her gaze.

'Would you mind if we asked Asako about this omurice directly?'

Takayuki gave only a troubled sigh in response.

'That's a no, then,' said Koishi, setting her pen back down.

'Well . . . I guess there might be no other way. Still, promise it'll be your last resort, okay?' Takayuki had lapsed into his native Saga accent, startling Koishi slightly.

'Absolutely. One last question. Why now? What made you want to eat the omurice *now*?'

'I'm trying to break the spell, if you see what I mean. Hisahiko has been kind enough to give me a job, but I'll only be there a couple more months. I'm planning to start a small company of my own by the summer. From now on, I want to live my life without constantly worrying about Shinji. You know, on my own terms.'

Koishi snapped her notebook shut. 'That makes sense. I'll get Dad on the case.'

Back in the restaurant, they found Nagare engrossed in the pages of a weekly magazine.

'Dad? We're done.'

Koishi's voice seemed to jolt him back to reality. 'Got all the details, then?' he asked.

Takayuki exchanged a glance with Koishi. 'Your daughter let me talk her ear off.'

'Dad, this could be Mr Jojima's chance at a fresh start in life. You have to go all out this time, okay?' Koishi clapped her father on the back so vigorously that the sound reverberated around the room.

'What do you mean *this* time?' he said with a wince. 'I always do.'

'Thank you very much,' said Takayuki, bowing in his direction.

Nagare bowed back. 'I'll get to the bottom of this.'

'When should I come back, then?'

'Usually takes us about two weeks. We'll be in touch.'

'Right. I'll be looking forward to it. Oh, and I owe you for lunch . . .' Takayuki opened his briefcase.

'You can pay later,' put in Koishi. 'Together with the detective fee.'

Takayuki closed the briefcase again, then pulled on his coat.

Nagare and Koishi followed him outside to see him off.

After watching his figure recede down Shomen-dori, they headed back inside.

'Never seen you so absorbed in one of those weeklies, Dad. Did an article catch your eye or something?'

'Actually, there was a feature on Mr Tsuda.'

'Ah. Good that he's doing so well for himself, don't you think?'

'What impresses me most is that part about arranging for his stepmother to move to Tokyo and live with him.'

'Funny, I never imagined one of his employees would come wandering through our door.'

'Speaking of which – what does Mr Jojima want us to find?'

'Omurice.'

'Interesting. Wouldn't have thought he was the type. I'm assuming there's a story behind it?'

'Yeah. Bit of a sad one. Or . . . well, it's complicated, let's put it that way.'

Koishi took a seat at one of the tables. Nagare sat down opposite her.

'You'd better fill me in.'

2

In spring, two weeks can make all the difference. By the time he returned to Kyoto, Takayuki didn't even need his coat. Clad instead in a beige cardigan, he made his way out of the station's Karasuma exit, and then north up the avenue of the same name.

As he turned east down Shomen-dori, he had to stifle a yawn. Since the pair had been in touch to arrange his second visit, he'd barely been able to sleep at night. One half of him was dying to get to the restaurant, while the other was reluctant to take another step. As a result, his pace was a little uneven.

'Are you a customer, too?' he said to the tabby cat he found by the entrance, squatting and scratching it behind the ears.

Koishi slid the door open and poked her head out. 'Good to see you again!'

'Does this cat live here?'

'Wouldn't quite put it that way. Dad never lets him inside.'

'Oh dear. Does he have a name?'

'Drowsy. Loves a snooze, you see. You won't catch him doing much else.'

'Easy life for some, isn't it?' Takayuki got to his feet and followed her inside where, still twitching nervously, he greeted Nagare.

'Don't you worry,' Koishi reassured him as she closed the door behind them. 'Dad has worked his usual magic.'

'It'll be ready in just a moment,' added Nagare, before disappearing back into the kitchen.

Takayuki took a seat, then gave an uncertain shrug. 'I can't quite decide whether I'm excited or terrified.'

'How many years will it be since you last ate it?' asked Koishi.

'Twenty-five. No . . .' Takayuki counted on his fingers, then gave a strained smile. 'Twenty-six.'

'Must have been hard to resist eating it all that time.' She poured him a cup of green tea. 'I mean, it was one of your favourite dishes, wasn't it?'

Takayuki took a long sip of the tea. 'Funnily enough, I've never even felt like it. It's like I mentally crossed it off the menu. About ten years ago, when I was served it at a work lunch, the mere sight of it turned my stomach. I mumbled something about an allergy and ordered curry instead.'

'Amazing how your subconscious can play tricks like that on you, isn't it? Your favourite dish, and now it makes you queasy . . . Well, I just hope you'll be alright today.'

'To be honest, I have no idea how I'll feel.'

As he set his teacup back down, Nagare arrived from the kitchen with a silver tray. On it, sitting on a white plate, was the omurice.

'Here we are.' He set the plate down in front of Takayuki, who leaned forward, transfixed.

'That's it, alright . . .'

'I'm pretty sure it'll be as you remember.' Nagare smiled confidently, then bowed. 'But let me know if anything's amiss.'

Koishi set a glass of water down, together with a flask for refills. Then, after exchanging a nod, the pair withdrew to the kitchen.

Takayuki reached for his spoon. Then he sat there, motionless, still staring at the omurice.

In his head, the hands of the clock were winding back at dizzying speed. Soon he could almost hear Asako's voice in the distance.

He raised his spoon and, aiming for the central, tomato-sauce-lathered part of the omelette that was draped over the rice, scooped out his first mouthful.

Determined to savour the taste, he tensed his mouth and, lips firmly closed, sat there chewing for some time. After a while, he began to experience a peculiar sensation. It was as though the many barbs that had lodged in his heart over the years were being removed, one by one, with every up-down motion of his jaw.

Takayuki found himself wondering, not for the first time in his life, whether a plate of food this delicious should even be allowed to exist in the world. What was it about this simple combination of rice, egg and tomato sauce that was causing these bittersweet emotions to well in his chest? This sadness? This almost unbearable pain?

He ate on in silence, attempting to detect some sort of hidden meaning in the omurice beyond its obvious deliciousness. Almost immediately, he understood this to be futile.

For all these years, he had somehow held the plate of food in front of him responsible for everything that had gone wrong in his life. Why? He tried to quell the frustration, the self-pity, the tears that were rising up from inside him – and failed. He saw clearly, now, that he had no one and nothing to blame but his own lack of courage. If he had spent all these years avoiding omurice, it was because he'd been afraid to confront that truth.

If he could – if he was only *allowed* – he'd want to go back to being the person he was before he ever tasted this dish. But that didn't stop his spoon from moving back and forth.

The tomato sauce did taste a little like ketchup, but it also carried a faint bitterness, even a sort of spiciness. The chicken rice, meanwhile, was fragrant and salty-sweet. There was no doubt in his mind: this was exactly how Asako had always made it for him.

His earlier emotions gave way to astonishment and confusion. Just how, exactly, had Nagare pulled this off?

To have tracked this exact dish down and recreated it perfectly, all within the space of two weeks, seemed an almost superhuman feat. With every mouthful, Takayuki's bewilderment only deepened.

'Tea?'

Koishi had arrived with a Karatsu-ware teapot and cup.

'Wait. Are those . . . ?'

'Let me guess. They remind you of Asako's.'

'I mean, I'm no ceramics expert, but they do look very familiar.' Takayuki took the cup in his hands. 'How did you . . .'

Koishi beamed. 'Dad's very detail-oriented.'

'Right.' He looked hesitantly up at her. 'Erm . . .'

'Yes?'

'I don't suppose I could get a . . . second helping?'

'Coming right up, mister!' Koishi paused, winced and gave a shy chuckle. 'Sorry, got a little carried away there.'

'Doesn't have to be a big portion. I'd just like to savour the taste a little longer.'

'That'll be music to Dad's ears.' Koishi hurried off to the kitchen.

Carefully, almost lovingly, Takayuki nibbled away at the small amount of egg and rice that remained on his plate.

'So I got it right, then?' said Nagare, setting an additional, smaller plate of omurice down alongside the first.

'Oh, yes. No doubt about that. It's exactly the same.'

'Glad to hear it.'

'How did you . . . ?'

'You finish up first, and then I'll tell you everything, I promise.' Nagare slipped his silver tray under one arm, then ducked back through the curtain into the kitchen.

When Takayuki had finished his first plate, he switched it for the second. This time, he ate even more slowly and deliberately. As he delighted in the aromas, and relished the flavours, he imagined the omurice travelling from his gut to his heart, where it would presumably remain for ever.

When had a meal left him feeling so deeply *content*, rather than simply full? So long ago, apparently, that he couldn't even remember.

The chicken tasted glorious, with none of the slightly gamey smell it sometimes had. Until he'd tasted Asako's omurice, he'd never even noticed the flavour of the chicken used in it. The rice would have been a fantastic meal in its own right. He remembered telling Asako as much – and the flash of honest joy, like that of a young girl, that had lit up her face afterwards.

'How are you getting on?' asked Nagare.

'It's incredible. I'm dying to know how you managed it.'

'Shall I get you some more?'

'Oh, no, I couldn't.' Takayuki rubbed his stomach. 'I haven't eaten this much in a long time.'

'Very good.'

'So – can you tell me how you did it?'

'Certainly.' Nagare took a seat opposite him.

'I don't mean to sound sceptical, but you . . . really didn't ask Asako directly, then?'

'No,' Nagare answered emphatically. 'You can trust me on that. I've never been very good at lying.'

'I lied to Dad once when I was little,' interjected Koishi as she refilled Takayuki's tea. 'About something tiny. I've never seen him so angry.'

'Sorry. It's just . . . you did such a flawless job.'

'Got my first lead from a TV show.' Nagare set a DVD down on the table. 'They were doing a special all-access feature on Shinji Kawanami's daily life. He didn't mention the omurice specifically, but they did ask him if there was any food he didn't like. Do you know what he said?'

'Hmm . . .' Takayuki had averted his gaze from the DVD. 'Food he didn't like . . . I don't remember ever noticing anything like that.'

'Parsley and celery. Apparently he can't even stand the smell of them.'

Takayuki shot the DVD a sideways glance. 'Those are two of my favourites!'

'I thought as much. Remember when I served you that bamboo rice last time, with the sansho pepper leaves? You mentioned that you liked those sorts of strong herbal flavours.'

'Come to think of it, Shinji never sprinkled sansho pepper

on his eel, either. Okay, so he doesn't like that sort of thing. But what's that got to do with the omurice?'

'You told us that whenever Shinji ate it anywhere else, he would polish it off in no time. It was only Asako's that he wouldn't finish. Meanwhile, you were so keen on it that it's stayed with you your whole life. I figured that must have something to do with your contrasting preferences when it came to flavours.'

'Right . . .'

'So I paid a visit to Karatsu.'

'You . . . went all that way?'

'Dad loves a good field trip,' explained Koishi, glancing at her father.

'Mr Kawanami's family no longer lived in his old home, but the building itself was still there. I asked around until I made the acquaintance of an elderly lady who'd been on good terms with Asako. People her age have the most amazing memories. She told me about Asako like it was yesterday.' Nagare produced a photo of the woman in question standing in front of the old Kawanami house.

'That's their house!' Takayuki smiled as he inspected the photo. 'Wow, this really does take me back. Though I don't think I ever met this woman.'

'You might not know her, but she'd heard all about you from Asako. How you were helping her son. How she thought of you as part of the family. And how you had a soft spot for her omurice.'

Takayuki's smile widened. 'She said that?'

'The two of them used to go shopping at the San'ei market – not far from that Takeya eel restaurant you mentioned. Good place for cheap, fresh fish, I'm told.'

'Really? Never even heard of it.'

'Just in front of the market, there's a trader who sells vegetables off a small trailer. Asako would drop by almost every Saturday and pick up some celery. When her friend asked her what she needed it for, she explained that it had a very special purpose.'

'The omurice?'

'See, she really did think of you as her own son. When she learned you liked herbal flavours, she decided to put celery in her omurice. But because her actual son wasn't partial to it, she had to hide it – by mashing it up and mixing it into her tomato sauce. You seemed pretty happy with the result – which is why she never stopped making it that way.'

'Incredible.' Takayuki dipped his finger into the tiny amount of tomato sauce that remained on his empty plate, then licked it clean.

'Opposite the market was a ceramics shop that Asako used to frequent. That's where I found this.' Nagare reached for the teapot.

'I knew I recognized it,' said Takayuki, cradling his matching cup with both hands.

'Something told me there was more to the recipe. You'd mentioned that the rice tasted oddly familiar, somehow. That seemed to indicate it wasn't just flavoured with ketchup. It must have contained some other ingredient – one you'd eaten from a young age.'

'Yes . . .' Takayuki's eyes glazed over slightly. 'It was like she'd added both ketchup and a flavour I'd always known.'

'Which, to me, had to mean something Japanese. I was wondering what that ingredient could have been when I learned that there was a restaurant nearby that served Western food, but also had Japanese-style rice bowls on the menu. So I headed there.'

'Never heard of anywhere like that. We didn't really eat out much in my family – mainly because we couldn't afford to.'

'Tsukamoto, the place is called. Run by an elderly couple. It's in the Watada neighbourhood now, but it used to be over by the town hall. They've picked up their fair share of regulars over the years. Now, they had omurice on the menu, as you might expect. But I also spotted tamago-don – as in, Japanese-style rice topped with soy-scrambled eggs. I tried them both. It's the sort of spot where you can do that and still get change from a thousand-yen note.'

'Dad's usually a light eater,' Koishi remarked, 'but you

know, when duty calls . . .' Takayuki smiled, nodded and waited for Nagare to go on.

'It's one of those casual places where they leave all the condiments out on the table. They even have soy sauce – not what you'd expect in a Western-style restaurant, but of course there are those rice bowls on the menu.'

'Soy sauce?' said Takayuki dubiously. 'That is unusual.'

'There was this older gentleman sitting next to me, and guess what? He was pouring it on his chicken rice, of all things. I assumed he must have picked up the wrong bottle by mistake, so I leaned over and told him: "That's soy sauce, you know."'

'And was your advice well received?'

'Turned out I'd been a little hasty. He told me he'd always eaten it that way. We left the restaurant at the same time, so I carried on chatting with him more. He mentioned that the soy sauce was made by a Karatsu-based company called Miyashita Shoyu.'

'Hmm. Sounds vaguely familiar.'

'It was proper Kyushu-style soy sauce – sweeter than usual.'

At a nod from Nagare, Koishi brought over a small bottle of the soy sauce in question. 'This stuff,' she explained.

'Ah, yes, I remember. We had it at home, too. Used to put it on everything.'

'When Asako had finished frying the chicken rice, she'd

season it with a splash of this. The result – as you noticed – was a flavour you could only describe as "familiar".'

'Do you think she knew it was a favourite of mine?'

'That I don't know, I'm afraid.'

'So they were the secret ingredients. Soy sauce and celery.'

'I thought it was pretty tasty too,' said Koishi. 'Even without the emotional attachment.'

Takayuki let out a deep sigh. 'This dish was where it all started to go wrong for me. Not that I'm blaming the omu-rice, obviously . . .'

'Listen, I can't speak for you, but I'm not so sure there's such a thing as going wrong in life. Or going right, for that matter.' Nagare looked steadily at Takayuki as he spoke. 'If you're making ends meet, not causing anyone too much hassle, and you make it to a decent age in one piece, I'd say that's a pretty decent life all told.'

Takayuki responded with another sigh, his eyes glued to the empty plate in front of him.

'I mean, I've caused plenty of hassle in my time,' Nagare continued, 'and I don't know if I have all that much to boast about, but still . . . Can't say I regret any of it. If I went around telling people my life was a failure, how could I ever look my family in the face?'

Koishi glanced at him, eyes glistening. 'That . . . means a lot, Dad.'

Takayuki got to his feet. 'Thank you both for everything.'

'You're free now,' grinned Nagare. 'You can eat all the omurice you like.'

Koishi held out a plastic folder. 'Here's the recipe, too – in case you fancy making it yourself.'

'Or maybe someone'll make it for you,' said Nagare.

Takayuki smiled sheepishly. 'That'll be the day.'

'Whatever happens,' said Koishi, 'you enjoy life, okay?'

'I'll try. Now, how much do I owe you?'

'Here are our details. Just send us however much feels right to you.' Koishi gave him a slip of paper, which he tucked into his wallet.

'Thank you again,' said Takayuki once they'd left the restaurant. He bowed deeply, gave Drowsy a quick scratch on the head, and set off down Shomen-dori.

As they watched him go, they couldn't help noticing how much lighter on his feet he seemed than when he'd arrived.

'Mr Jojima!' Nagare called.

Takayuki turned. 'Yes?'

'Life's what we make of it. You hear me?'

'Oh yes. Loud and clear!'

'Did *you* ever have a rival, Dad?' asked Koishi once they were back inside.

'Plenty. Back in my student days, and when I worked as a chef. Oh, and in the police, of course.'

'What about when you were in love? Was there anyone else vying for Mum's affection?'

Nagare looked up from the table he was wiping, then glanced towards the family altar. 'You'll have to ask her that yourself.'

'Oh, there definitely was. Wasn't there, Mum?' Koishi made her way over to the altar and, pressing her hands together in prayer, gazed up at her mother's photo.

'Something tells me she might have regretted her choice. Really let her down in the end, didn't I . . .'

Nagare lit a stick of incense, then bowed his head apologetically. But Koishi was shaking her head in disagreement.

Chapter 6:
Croquettes

1

As she crossed Karasuma-dori, heading away from Higashi Honganji temple, Miyuki Akikawa passed a monk hurrying the other way. It was December, after all – the season when the temples were famously busy with all sorts of ceremonies, as well as the all-important yearly cleaning. The leafless branches of the large ginkgo trees swayed in the winter wind.

Kyoto was known for its cold winters, when a penetrating chill seemed to rise up from the very ground. Miyuki might as well have been walking across a layer of ice – though, as it happened, she was making her way across a golden carpet of fallen ginkgo leaves. As she buttoned the collar of her white coat and hunched herself against the wind, she found herself wondering why on earth she'd opted for a skirt.

Walking east, it wasn't long until she found herself standing outside a building that matched the description she'd been given.

'Guess this is it,' she murmured, before reaching a hand towards the door.

Just then, though, it abruptly slid open.

'See you next time!' declared a voice, and out strolled a young man, causing Miyuki to back away slightly.

'Oops!' said the man with a chuckle. 'Sorry if I gave you a fright.' He hurried off down the street.

Miyuki pulled the door open once more and walked inside.

Inside, a woman in a black sommelier's apron turned to greet her. 'Hello!'

'Is this the Kamogawa Diner?'

'It is. Can I help you?'

'Is it . . . also the Kamogawa Detective Agency?'

'So that's what you're here for. Koishi Kamogawa – head of the agency.'

'Miyuki Akikawa. Nice to meet you.' Miyuki bowed her head.

'Take a seat. How hungry are you?'

'I'd love to eat something, if you're serving.' Miyuki sat down on one of the folding chairs and glanced around, taking in the restaurant's interior.

'Mind leaving the menu up to me?' asked a man in chef's whites who had appeared from the kitchen.

'I'm officially in charge of the agency, but Dad here does all the legwork,' explained Koishi. 'His name's Nagare Kamogawa.'

Miyuki got to her feet again and introduced herself with a bow.

'Anything you're not so keen on?' asked Nagare.

'I'm not too good with strong flavours. Otherwise, anything's fine.'

'Fragrant herbs, that sort of thing?'

'No, more like fermented fish. Or sea squirt.'

'Then you don't have to worry. We don't serve anything like that!' With a parting grin, Nagare went back into the kitchen.

'Where have you come from today, then?' asked Koishi, setting a teacup down on the table.

'Tokyo.'

Koishi paused as she poured green tea into the cup. 'Do I know you from somewhere?'

'I . . . think I just have one of those faces,' replied Miyuki, glancing away.

Koishi cocked her head to one side. 'Right. You're . . . sure?'

Miyuki gave a little smile. 'Positive.'

'Well, what can I get you to drink?'

'Sake would be perfect.'

'Chilled? Or shall I warm some up? It *is* cold out there.'

'I prefer chilled, thanks.'

'Anything in mind?'

'Just something dry, please.'

'I'll get Dad to pick you one out.' Koishi hurried off to the kitchen.

Alone now at the table, Miyuki gave the restaurant another once-over.

She had almost no memories of eating out as a child, but her mother had taken her to a shokudo-style restaurant once, and it had looked a lot like this one. A little shelf hanging down from the ceiling, on which sat a small television and a miniature shrine. The laminated tables, gleaming under the lights, and on one of them a folded newspaper. All she really remembered was how good the udon had tasted – though that might have had more to do with how happy she'd been to be eating out with her mother in the first place.

Nagare appeared with a tray full of food. 'Sorry to keep you waiting.'

'This looks . . . incredible,' murmured Miyuki, gazing at the array of dishes he had begun arranging on the table.

'Oh, it's nothing too fancy. I've focused on warm dishes, given the wintry weather.'

When he'd finished, there were eight small plates, dishes and bowls in front of her.

'I've never . . . eaten anything like this before.' Miyuki's eyes filled with wonder as they darted from dish to dish.

'Shall I talk you through it?'

Miyuki sat up in her seat. 'Please.'

'I'll start in the top left. That small Shigaraki dish is bo-
dara, simmered in soy sauce, with an ebi-imo taro puree.
Next to that, on the Oribe plate, is grilled tilefish – tasty
with a squeeze of kabosu. In the little pot there you'll find
the scales from the fish, deep-fried for extra crunch. The
lidded bowl in the top right is boiled Shogoin daikon radish,
served with two types of miso: the red one is Hatcho, while
the sweeter white one is Saikyo. Below that, on the little
Imari dish, are the sake-steamed hamaguri clams. Sprinkle
some grated yuzu peel on those if you like. In the middle is
Seko crab, also steamed. It'll be tasty enough as it is, or you
could try adding a dash of the mustard-infused vinegar. To
the left of that, in the Bizen bowl, is a Western-style beef
stew – served with grilled wheat-gluten cake instead of the
usual bread. And below, in the bottom left on the Kutani
plate, is the deep-fried fugu. It's already seasoned, but feel
free to sprinkle over a little extra sansho pepper. Finally,
bottom right, in the lacquered bowl is oyster simmered in
a soy-milk broth. Nice with a sprinkle of grated cheese and
the kuro-shichimi spice blend.'

'I've . . . no idea where to even start. Is there an order
I'm supposed to eat all this in?'

Just looking at the right dish had been challenging
enough. Most of Nagare's actual explanation had gone in
one ear and out the other.

'Oh, just eat whatever you like, however you like. Now,

how about this sake? Suigei, from Kochi prefecture. The "Drunken Whale".' He handed her the bottle.

'Thank you. I like sake, but I don't know the first thing about it.'

'Well, it's the same as the food: drink it however you like. That's really all there is to it.' Nagare bowed, then returned to the kitchen.

As a hush fell over the restaurant, Miyuki sat there alone in front of the food. She cleared her throat quietly. Where to start? Part of her wanted to get this right; part of her couldn't care less. These days, people tended to assume she was something of a gourmand, but the truth was she'd spent a much longer portion of her life staring hunger in the face than savouring fine cuisine. It was a side of herself she rarely felt able to reveal – but here, there was no need to hide anything. With a relieved sigh, she set her chopsticks down and reached for one of the hamaguri clams with her fingers.

Though she picked up her chopsticks again when it came to scooping the flesh from inside the shell, even the most dexterous fiddling failed to dislodge the chewy ligament. This time, after a quick glance around to ensure no one was watching, she swapped the chopsticks for her teeth.

It tasted so good that she let out a quiet gasp. Grasping her chopsticks once more, she moved on to what Nagare had called the bo-dara.

Of course, she hadn't had a clue what that actually

meant – or the presence of mind to ask. If the 'dara' part meant 'cod', then presumably that was the fish in front of her. It looked like it had been dried first, and then simmered in soy sauce as Nagare had said. Miyuki wasn't quite sure whether coming face to face with all these dishes she'd never even laid eyes on as a child was making her *happy*, exactly. But what she did know was that sitting here, gazing at them while she sipped on the chilled sake, felt somehow enriching for her soul.

Next, she tried some of the little fried things in the small pot. It took her a moment to realize that they were fish scales. Remembering that they'd come from what Nagare had said was a tilefish, she crunched slowly on them, savouring the subtle yet rich flavours that filled her mouth. By now, Miyuki's expression had softened into a smile.

'How are you getting on?' asked Nagare, arriving at her side with another bottle of sake.

'It's all so good,' said Miyuki, dabbing at her mouth with a handkerchief. 'You know, I've hardly even eaten any of these things before!'

'Glad to hear it. Thought I'd bring you through a different sake to try. Sake Hitosuji, it's called, from Bizen. Made using Omachi rice, and pairs nicely with milder dishes like the ones I've served you today. Give it a try if you like.'

Nagare placed the green bottle on the table with a glass, then retreated back into the kitchen.

Miyuki unscrewed the bottle's cap, filled the small glass and set it down alongside the sake she was already drinking. They looked exactly the same to her. It was only after taking a few sips from each and comparing them that she began to notice the differences. Once she'd finished both, she picked up her chopsticks again and reached for the crab.

She seasoned the flaky meat with the mustard vinegar and slipped it into her mouth. Almost immediately, she pinched her nose and stifled a sneeze.

'Oops. Too much vinegar.' She chuckled to herself as she dabbed the tears from her eyes with her handkerchief.

She worked her way through the oyster, Shogoin daikon, and deep-fried fugu, pausing only to empty and refill her sake glass. Before long, her cheeks had taken on a rosy flush.

'Shall I bring you some rice?' asked Nagare, who had arrived behind her at some point.

'Oh. I didn't know there'd be rice, too . . .' Miyuki pressed the palms of her hands against her cheeks. 'I've gone and made myself a little tipsy.'

'I'll make it a small portion,' said Nagare as he returned to the kitchen.

'Some chilled water, maybe?' Koishi set a glass down on the table, together with a flask for refills.

'Thank you!' exclaimed Miyuki, immediately draining the glass.

'You *do* like a drink, don't you!' Koishi caught Miyuki's eye, and the pair chuckled.

As Koishi went off to prepare for their interview, Nagare returned from the kitchen enveloped in a cloud of steam.

'Today's rice is steamed with unagi eel. It's hot, so be careful.' He set a small, square wooden steamer on the table. Steam billowed from under its lid. 'Might be a little tricky to eat with chopsticks, so I'll leave you a spoon too.'

As he retreated once more, Miyuki gripped the wooden spoon he'd given her and scooped up a mouthful from the middle of the box.

The brown, sauce-infused rice was covered with strips of eel, themselves sprinkled with a delicate layer of finely chopped omelette. She blew on her spoon, then cautiously eased it into her mouth. Even so, as she began chewing away, she found herself opening her mouth wide in order to let cool air in.

'That *is* hot,' she murmured once she'd managed to swallow the rice.

She was already full – and yet the hand holding her spoon kept moving. As she continued to wolf down the rice, Miyuki began to feel the familiar stirrings of self-loathing.

'Watch you don't burn your mouth,' said Nagare, refilling her glass with water from the flask.

Miyuki set her spoon down. 'Sorry. Eating like a pig, aren't I? How embarrassing . . .'

'Oh, please. Wouldn't taste as good any other way, would it? This sort of grub was made to be eaten like that. And there's nothing a chef likes to see more than someone relishing their food.'

'That's very kind of you. I've never been the daintiest person, you see.' Miyuki drained the glass of water and set it down on the table.

'All that matters is that you enjoy the meal. Now, when you've had a moment to digest, I'll show you through to Koishi.'

'Sorry for dawdling,' said Miyuki, wiping her mouth with her handkerchief and making as if to get up.

'There's no rush at all. Can I bring you some hot tea first?'

'No, I'm fine.' Miyuki got to her feet and composed herself slightly. 'Please – show me through.'

As she made her way down the long corridor, Miyuki kept pausing to gaze at the patchwork of photos on its walls.

'Things I've cooked over the years,' said Nagare over his shoulder. 'The photos are so I don't forget.'

'Is this a bowl of udon? You don't just do Kyoto dishes, then?'

'My wife loved her noodles. Actually, by the end, udon

194

was about all she *could* eat.' Nagare turned and carried on walking.

'The one time my mother took me out for a meal, it was for udon. Since then, having it at a restaurant has always seemed like the ultimate treat . . .' Miyuki's voice echoed down the corridor, though she seemed to be addressing herself more than anyone else.

Nagare showed her into the office, then turned back down the corridor.

'Please, take a seat,' said Koishi, gesturing towards the sofa opposite her. 'Now, if you could just fill this out . . .'

Miyuki whipped through the form, then slid it back across the low table.

'Miyuki Akikawa. Occupation: writer. Is that for a magazine or something?' Koishi asked without looking up from the form.

'I write books, actually.'

'Ooh. As in . . . novels?'

'Yes, you could call them that.'

Koishi glanced up. 'What sort?'

'Romantic fiction, mainly,' replied Miyuki, her own gaze dropping to the table.

'Those are my favourite! Do you write under your real name?'

'No.' Miyuki drew in her shoulders slightly. 'I have a pen name. Aki-Miyu.'

Koishi gaped at her. 'Wait. You're *the* Aki-Miyu?'

Miyuki covered her face with her hands. 'Sorry, I get shy when people stare at me . . .'

'So this is what you look like when you're not in character! I guess that makes sense – I mean, you can't go around looking like *that* all the time.'

'That was my publisher's idea,' explained Miyuki, staring into her own lap. 'They talked me into dressing like that when I made my debut, and it sort of stuck.'

'What a transformation, though. I always imagined you as this sort of vixen, and yet here you are, all polite and neatly dressed.'

'I was never really that keen on those outfits. But that's the Aki-Miyu everyone has come to expect. Not much I can do about it now.'

'I mean, your novels *do* get pretty spicy . . . But you even talk differently. Is that all part of the act?'

Miyuki nodded silently in response.

'And here I was thinking writers had it easy.' Koishi sighed, then opened her notebook. 'Anyway, what's this dish you're looking for?'

There was a pause. Then, in an even quieter voice than before, Miyuki replied: 'Croquettes.'

Koishi had to stifle a giggle. 'Sorry. I know I shouldn't laugh. It's just . . . the idea that the person behind all those passionate love stories is out on a quest for croquettes, of all things. I don't quite get it, but I love it.'

Miyuki's face finally relaxed into a smile. 'Not quite what you'd expect, is it?'

'I really didn't mean to laugh, I promise. Now, could you tell me a bit more about these croquettes?'

'Actually, it gets more embarrassing. Or . . . shameful, I should say.'

Koishi leaned forward, waiting for her to go on. But Miyuki simply sat there, her expression frozen.

'You can skip over anything you'd rather not talk about,' offered Koishi.

'Thank you. But I think I have to give you the whole story if I want your help.' Miyuki sat up, composed herself, and went on. 'I was what you might call a wayward young girl. It must have started when I was ten or so – acting out, only going to school when I felt like it, that kind of thing.'

'Bit of a rebel, then.'

'It was just my mother and me at home. We lived hand to mouth. Looking back, I know that's no excuse, but at the time I couldn't help wondering why I was the only one who had to put up with all that. I was just so fed up with the life we had.'

'Looking at you now, I'd never have even begun to imagine . . .'

'Mum was always at her part-time job. After school I'd

come back to an empty home. She'd only get back after seven in the evening, by which time I'd be ravenous.'

'Nothing worse than an empty belly when you're a kid. Sounds like your mother had it pretty tough too, though.'

'I wanted to tell her that slaving away like that wasn't going to solve anything. She could have signed us up for welfare, found a better-paying job. But she chose to do neither. I asked her about it once, right after I'd started middle school. She just muttered something about how the person she was working for had done her a favour. In any case, *I* was the one who suffered as a result.' Miyuki was speaking breathlessly now, her expression lapsing into a frown.

'For a kid, it sounds like you had a pretty good handle on the world.'

'Coming from a home like that, I hardly had any friends, so instead I'd spend my days reading books I borrowed from the library. I think my mother just thought I was a bit of a know-it-all.'

'But . . . you had a soft spot for her croquettes?'

'No,' Miyuki shot back immediately. 'Not hers.'

Koishi was taken aback. 'Then . . . whose?'

'Listen, I know she was strapped for cash, but all my mother seemed to cook was boiled vegetables, miso soup, and stir fries with the tiniest smattering of meat. She never made me anything as indulgent as a croquette. Which was why . . .'

Miyuki trailed off as though lost for words, her eyes drifting back to the low table. Koishi waited with bated breath for her to go on.

The silence must have lasted less than a minute, but with all the freshly awakened memories that were swirling around Miyuki's head, it felt to her like a very long time. Eventually, she took a deep breath and, as if steeling herself, went on.

'I . . . stole them.'

Whatever Koishi had been expecting, it wasn't this. She was too stunned to even think of a response.

'There was this butcher's shop on the way home from school,' Miyuki continued. 'And in the vacant lot next to it, this old lady ran a little croquette stall, all by herself. It wasn't just the usual meat-and-potato croquettes, either. She sold all sorts of things. Pork cutlets, mincemeat patties, chunks of ham – all deep-fried in breadcrumbs. There was always a queue. I mean, it's not like there were any other croquette sellers in our neighbourhood.'

'Few and far between these days, aren't they?' said Koishi, relieved to have found something to say. 'Though, actually, there's one just around the corner from here.'

'Whenever I walked past, this amazing smell would waft over. Pulling me in like a magnet. The old lady was always chatting away to her customers. While they had her attention, I'd snatch two of the little croquettes and shove them in my pocket.'

'Right. So . . . this wasn't just a one-time thing.'

'No. I was what you'd call a repeat offender.' Miyuki's face creased into a smile of self-derision.

'And she never caught you?'

'She was just so wrapped up in her chatter. And I was short for my age. With all the customers in the way, I don't think she could even see me.'

'Did you eat them at home?'

'Yes. I'd run the whole way home, lock the door, shut the curtains and gobble them down. They always tasted incredible.'

'You didn't add the usual sauce?'

'There was no time for that. I just shoved them straight into my mouth.'

'Must have tasted a little plain, then.'

'That's the strange part. When I eat croquettes these days, they always need the sauce. But those ones were delicious just the way they were. Anyway, I was in a rush to finish them because I wanted to destroy the evidence. You know, remove all traces of my crime.'

'So even as a kid, you knew you'd done something bad?'

'Oh, sure, I knew stealing was wrong. But there was no arguing with my empty stomach.'

'You really were hungry, then.'

Miyuki gave a small nod. 'It's funny, now that I look back

on it. There I was, stealing food every day, and no one even noticed.'

'You're sure the old woman didn't see you?'

'Oh, absolutely. I'd walk past her stall on my way to school the next morning, and she'd smile and say hello.'

'Don't take this the wrong way,' said Koishi with a slight grin, 'but it sounds like you were a bit of a natural.'

'You might be right. And somehow that made me feel less guilty about the whole thing. Soon it became a habit – in fact, it even gave me a bit of a thrill. Awful, I know. Before I knew it, I was pinching things from other places, too. I'd become a serial shoplifter.'

'Someone must have caught you eventually.'

'Oh yes. At first I got off with a warning or two, but after that they sent me to a correctional facility.'

'Must have been tough on your mother, too.'

'Whenever she came to visit me, she'd burst into tears,' said Miyuki in a detached tone. 'You know, apologizing. Saying it was all her fault.'

'Poor her,' murmured Koishi.

'*She's* the one you feel sorry for?' asked Miyuki with a frown. 'You're trying to tell me my mother is the one who deserves sympathy here?'

'No, but . . . I mean, it's not like she chose to fall on hard times, is it?'

'Listen, I don't care what sort of obligation she was under

with that job of hers; the truth is she was sacrificing her child's happiness to save her own face. Tell me, is that what mothers are supposed to do?' By now, tears were trickling down Miyuki's cheeks, but she wasn't finished. 'You try being brought up by someone like that. The pain . . . the despair . . . the sheer *wretchedness* of it.'

'I . . . don't even know what to say,' said Koishi. She really didn't.

'Sorry. Getting a little worked up.' Miyuki dabbed at her eyes with a handkerchief, tucked it into her bag, then went on. 'I suppose we should get back to those croquettes . . .'

'Could you tell me the name of the stall, and where it was?' Koishi asked, notebook ready in her hand.

'It was so long ago that my memory's a little hazy. I don't think it's there any more, either.'

'Of course. I mean, if it was, you could just go and buy yourself one.'

'Back then, my mother and I lived in Kawasaki, not far from the famous Daishi temple.'

'Do you know the address?'

'Well, the neighbourhood was Daishi Ekimae – by the station. I'm not sure of the exact address, though.'

'Are there any landmarks that come to mind? For example, any parks nearby?'

'There was a clinic opposite our house. A nursery school, too. Oh, and a shrine. I think the croquette stall was on

Goriyaku-dori, which I used to walk along on my way home from school. The name of the butcher's shop started with "Matsu", I think. I don't remember the stall itself having a name.'

'Shouldn't be too tricky to find the butcher's. But this is' – Koishi glanced at Miyuki's age on the form – 'twenty years ago, isn't it? I wonder if the croquette lady is still around . . .'

'I don't know how old she is exactly, but even back then she must have been in her seventies.'

'Making her ninety-something now. Doesn't seem likely she's still selling croquettes.'

Miyuki's expression darkened. 'No, it doesn't . . .'

'Can I ask you something?'

'Go ahead.'

'It's about your mother. Are you . . .'

'I've broken off all contact with her,' Miyuki replied flatly. 'Don't even know if she's still alive. I haven't set foot in Kawasaki for years.'

Koishi glanced away for a moment, then changed the subject. 'What made you decide you wanted to eat one of these croquettes again, after all this time?'

'A book of mine's been nominated for a big award,' said Miyuki in a calm voice. 'They're announcing the winner in the spring. I don't want to count my chickens before they hatch, but if I *do* win, people are going to dig up all sorts about my past. It won't take long for them to learn about my days as a delinquent. And I'm fine with that. I mean, it's only the truth. And I paid my debt to society at the correctional facility. Paid for everything I stole, too. With one exception: the croquettes I took from that old lady's stall.'

'The media do like to dig the dirt on people when they win awards. But if no one ever caught you stealing the croquettes, what's there to uncover?'

'You're probably right. I guess it's more about finding some sort of closure. And if the old lady is still alive, I'd like to pay her back.'

'Got it. Well, I'll make sure Dad searches high and low.'

Miyuki got to her feet and bowed. 'Thank you very much.'

As they re-entered the restaurant, Nagare reached for the remote control and switched off the television.

'How was that, then?'

'She told me all about it, Dad. The next part's up to you.'

Miyuki bowed to each of them in turn. 'Thank you. When should I come back?'

'Would two weeks suit?' asked Koishi.

'Yes, that's fine. I'll try and brace myself . . . Now, how much was that meal?'

Nagare smiled. 'You can pay for it later, together with the detective fee.'

'If you insist,' said Miyuki, returning a glittering, silver-sequin-covered purse to her bag.

'I see your purse is still in character,' Koishi remarked.

'Yep. I brought the wrong one . . .'

The pair grinned at each other, while Nagare looked on in confusion.

'I'll be counting down the days.' Miyuki bowed once more, then slid the door open.

'So, what's the dish?' asked Nagare once they'd seen her off.

'Croquettes.'

'Homemade?'

'No. From a stall.'

'Do you know which?'

'Shouldn't be too hard to track down.'

'Whereabouts?'

'Kawasaki.'

'Ah, Kawasaki. Haven't been there in ages.'

'You've been before?'

'Your mother and I went there not long after we married. Visited Daishi temple.'

'Oh. Then it's in the same neck of the woods.'

'Feel like coming along? The temple sells these amulets that are meant to absorb misfortune.'

'I'm sold,' said Koishi, gripping his arm.

'Kikuko bought one. Used to take it everywhere with her.'

'Oh! The one that says "sacrificial talisman"?'

'That's the one.' Nagare glanced at the altar in the corner. Koishi smiled. 'I'll have to get one too, then.'

2

Kyoto was awash with warm sunlight. The weather could change so swiftly in a week or two that it was little wonder the traditional calendar was divided into twenty-four miniature seasons. Kyoto had a way of showcasing each and every one of them.

Maybe I should set my next novel here, thought Miyuki as she made her way across Karasuma-dori.

She stopped in front of the restaurant to remove her thin, peppermint-green coat, then slid the door open.

'Welcome back!' came Koishi's cheerful voice.

'Been quite warm recently, hasn't it?' said Miyuki as she hung her coat on a hook.

'Still cold enough in the mornings and evenings. I can't sleep without a hot water bottle!'

'That's adorable. I didn't know people still used those.'

'Well, Dad likes doing things the old-fashioned way,' said Koishi, glancing towards the kitchen.

'Is that a crime?' asked Nagare, poking his head through the curtain. He turned to Miyuki. 'Thanks for coming back. I'll get frying – just give me a moment.'

'Thank you,' said Miyuki, settling into one of the now-familiar folding chairs.

Koishi set about making some tea. 'I went with him, you know. To Kawasaki.'

'Not much to see, is there?'

'Oh, we had fun. That Daishi temple is really something. Went to the shrine near your old house, too. Heard about an unusual festival they hold there.' Koishi gave her a knowing look as she poured the tea. 'Something about . . . fertility? With lots of . . . erm, symbols?'

'Oh, that,' said Miyuki, blushing. 'I had no idea what it was about as a child. Of course, when I got a little older, it was all a little embarrassing . . .'

'Kawasaki's a big place, isn't it? Even the station's enormous. Makes Kyoto seem like a little village.'

Miyuki took a careful sip of her tea. 'Yes, I hear it's really mushroomed. I haven't been back in so long. When I was a kid it felt like this sleepy little backwater.'

Soon an appetizing aroma came drifting over from the kitchen. Miyuki could hear the sizzle of hot oil, too.

Koishi's own belly rumbled. 'What is it about deep-fried

food? I already tried a sample earlier, but now I feel like eating them all over again . . .'

'The smell . . .' said Miyuki, her eyes shut tight. 'It's exactly the same.'

Nagare returned with a small white plate. On it were two freshly fried croquettes.

'You ate these as a sort of . . . finger food, didn't you? That's why I haven't given you any rice or anything. I'd like you to enjoy them just as they are.'

Miyuki's eyes were open again now – and wide. 'But these are . . .'

'The croquette seller was three hundred and thirty metres from your house. For a kid running at full tilt, we're talking about a three- or four-minute dash. And if the croquettes were already sitting on a shelf at the stall, they can't have been fresh from the fryer when you took them. These came out two minutes ago, so I'd recommend giving it another three or so before you eat them. Maybe you could spend the time trying to remember how you felt back then.' With this advice, Nagare departed for the kitchen, followed by Koishi.

Left alone in the restaurant, Miyuki closed her eyes and let her mind wander back to those days.

The moment she left the school gates, she'd have only one destination in mind. She'd count the streets, one by one, until she reached the sixth, Goriyaku-dori. Turning the corner, she'd spot two small crowds of people. One in front of the butcher's, and one in front of the croquette stall.

Soon enough the old lady's loud voice would come into earshot, and she'd see the weathered face grimacing amid the oily smoke that filled the tiny stall. Wielding a long pair of chopsticks, the croquette seller would transport one deep-fried morsel after another from the fryer onto a large tray.

The customers, mainly middle-aged women, would shout out their own orders – asking for *this* many croquettes, *that* many patties, and so on. While some waited for their order to come out of the fryer, others would use a pair of tongs to transfer items from the tray to one of the little envelopes provided. There was a whole mountain of things to choose from – croquettes, deep-fried chunks of ham, even karaage chicken. As the tongs moved back and forth above her, Miyuki would wait patiently for the right moment. Then, quick as a flash, she'd snatch two croquettes from the pile closest to her and thrust them into her pocket. After that, it was simply a matter of charging home as fast as she could.

Had it been three minutes?

Miyuki looked back down at the croquettes. Was this really them? They looked a little different from your average croquette. But the smell wafting up from them was undeniably the one she remembered.

After holding a hand to them to check they were still faintly warm, she picked one up and took a bite.

There was no time to linger over the flavour. She simply chewed a few times, then swallowed.

Yes, this is it. This is the taste.

If I ever write a novel about all this, she thought, already reaching for the second croquette, *those'll be my opening sentences.*

Could any other croquettes ever compare to these? Miyuki knew that it wasn't just nostalgia making her feel this way. These croquettes tasted so good they didn't even need any sauce. And she had stolen them. The more she chewed, the more guilt seemed to gnaw at her own chest.

'How are they, then? Just as you remembered?' asked Nagare, who had appeared at her side.

'Oh, this is them, alright. It's funny, though. I remembered them being more . . . croquette-like. My memory must have been a bit fuzzy.'

'That part surprised me, too. I mean, they *are* technically croquettes, but they're a little unusual-looking.'

'Do you think I could . . . have some more?'

'Oh, please. How about I bring you some rice this time, too?'

'That would be . . . fantastic. I've actually always wondered what it'd be like to eat them like that. You know, as an actual meal.'

'Give me a minute. There's a freshly steamed pot waiting next door.' Nagare hurried back into the kitchen.

This was even more than Miyuki had dared to hope for. When she'd wolfed down the croquettes as a child, she'd often wished she'd had some hot rice to go with them. At home, the rice was usually cold, as were the boiled vegetables. The pot of miso soup could be reheated on the gas cooker, but otherwise dinner had been a pretty miserable affair. Now, she would finally get to eat the combination she'd always dreamed of: the croquettes and a bowl of hot rice.

'They're a good match, I can tell you that,' said Nagare, licking his lips as he brought over a black clay pot, set it down in front of Miyuki, and removed the lid.

Turning his face away from the mass of steam that rose from the pot, he scooped some of the rice into a Koimari bowl. Miyuki watched with an almost childlike wonder.

'There we go. Nice big portion.'

He set down a small bowl heaped high with pristine white rice. Thin wisps of steam snaked up from between the glistening grains.

Miyuki took the bowl in her hands and gave it a deep sniff.

'Smells . . . amazing.'

Next, Nagare brought the croquettes over on a plate.

Five of them this time, arranged neatly on a bed of shredded cabbage – together with a small bottle of brown liquid.

'You might want to try adding a bit of sauce this time – now that you have the rice to go with them, I mean. Enjoy!'

Miyuki wasted no time. She reached for one of the croquettes with her chopsticks and set it on top of the rice. Then she scooped it up with some of the steaming white grains and took a bite. It tasted incredible.

For some reason, she was reminded of how she felt when she'd come face to face with her first book, fresh off the press. She'd written the thing, so it shouldn't have felt like such a surprise. But the simple act of *seeing* it had sent a wave of merry excitement through her.

But . . . why was she feeling like that now?

She finished the first croquette and moved on to the second. It was as she reached for the third that the answer came to her.

It was because the dish was finally complete. It was because after all these years, she was finally enjoying them the way she was meant to.

The croquettes she'd stolen on an almost daily basis had been no more than one part of a greater whole. Shoving them into your mouth without even sitting down was one thing, but when you ate them at the table like this, with white rice to accompany each mouthful – that was when they reached their full potential. An obvious truth, really, but one it had taken her all this time to realize.

If she hadn't stolen them, they would have ended up on someone else's dining table, bringing someone else the rush of pure happiness she'd just experienced. With a fresh shudder of guilt, it dawned on her that she had been committing not just one crime, but two.

What was most pitiful of all was the fact that, for all the remorse she was feeling right now, her chopsticks were still moving. The croquettes were just too delicious.

In no time at all, she had devoured all five of them, plus the mountain of rice. It was only as she set her chopsticks back down that she noticed another bowl on the table, its contents obscured by a lid.

She lifted the lid and steam rushed out. Miso soup. She could see strips of wakame seaweed floating in it, as well as a few small chunks of tofu that had sunk to the bottom.

Miyuki felt a pang of nostalgia. It looked just like the soup she'd so often reheated as a child. When she took a sip she found herself recognizing the slightly salty taste, too. This had been the one dish where she could feel her mother's warmth.

'Well, you polished those off,' grinned Nagare, eyeing the empty plate and rice bowl.

Miyuki replaced the lid on the soup bowl and smiled back. 'They were so, so good.'

Nagare gestured to the chair opposite her. 'Can I sit with you for a moment?'

'Of course. I'm dying to hear how you managed this.' Miyuki waited for Koishi to clear the table, then pulled her own chair forward slightly.

'Well, it was obvious we needed to head to Kawasaki,' began Nagare. 'So off we went.'

Miyuki raised herself from her seat and bowed. 'Sorry to make you go all that way.'

'Actually, we were glad to have an excuse to visit Daishi temple. It's a special place for the two of us, you see. And you lived just around the corner. Almost like it was meant to be.'

'That does make me feel better.'

'You might already know this, but your old house is gone. Replaced by a three-storey apartment block.'

'Right,' replied Miyuki airily. 'I didn't know, actually.'

'As we'd expected, the croquette stall was gone too. These days, it's Matsuki-ya, the butcher's shop, that sells them.'

'Oh,' said Miyuki, her gaze dropping to the floor.

'But Mr Matsuki, the butcher, told me all about the old days. Your croquette seller's name was Tamayo Morita.'

'Tamayo Morita . . .' She looked up at him hesitantly. 'Do you know if she's still . . .'

Nagare slowly shook his head. Miyuki felt her shoulders sag in response.

'Her stall was so popular that some customers would even make the trip out from Tokyo. Morita Croquettes, people used to call it.'

Nagare produced an old sepia-toned photo and placed it in front of Miyuki. It showed a tiny stall on the empty plot of land by the butcher's shop, around which a gaggle of middle-aged women had formed.

'Yes,' murmured Miyuki, eyes widening as she leaned in. 'That's the place.'

'This photo is practically all that's left of it.'

'How precious.' Miyuki picked it up and straightened out its creased corners.

'Mrs Morita was the butcher's aunt. He'd sell her various cuts of meat and mincemeat wholesale, and she'd turn them into croquettes and things at her stall. Speaking of which, it turns out there were two types of croquette. One was the regular kind, flat and oval, like you find everywhere. The other was the one you were after. Stubby little barrel-shaped things.'

'Really? There were . . . two types?'

'You might not remember, but the croquettes were arranged on two shelves. The regular ones were at the top, while these barrel-shaped ones were at the bottom. In other words, just low enough that even a child could reach them. At least, that's how Mr Matsuki remembered it.'

Miyuki smiled slightly. 'I guess I only had eyes for the ones right in front of me.'

'As you'll have realized just now, the croquettes you were looking for were quite unusual. The ingredients – potato, onion and minced meat – are the same as a regular croquette, but there's no breadcrumb coating. Turns out they were the product of chance.'

'The product of . . . chance?'

'Mrs Morita's croquettes were so popular that one day, she ran out of breadcrumbs. But she still had the other ingredients, so she decided there was nothing for it but to coat them in potato starch instead, like you would a piece of karaage chicken. The result went down so well with customers that it became a permanent addition to the menu.'

'So they were a sort of . . . happy accident?'

'Other than the lack of breadcrumbs, they were basically the same as the regular croquettes. The only other difference was that she boosted the seasoning – the reason being that without the breadcrumb coating, it was hard to cover them with sauce. So she marinated the mincemeat in the sauce overnight instead. Started calling them the Tamayo Special – and they sold like nobody's business.'

'If the stall was so popular, I'm guessing it was illness or something that made her shut the place down?'

'Mrs Morita was closing up one day when she had a heart attack. She survived, but that was the end of her croquette business. She fought her illness for many years until, just last month, she passed away.'

'If only I'd come here a little sooner . . . Does she have any family?'

'A son, apparently, but he's unreachable.'

Miyuki bit her lip. 'I wanted to at least repay her.'

'About that. See, back then, the regular croquettes were thirty yen a pop. The Tamayo Special was only twenty-five, seeing as she skipped the breadcrumbs.'

Nagare opened a battered old notebook on the table. Inside, a sort of ledger had been drawn up using a pencil, with columns listing various dates, quantities and prices.

Miyuki studied the notebook, then looked up with a puzzled expression. 'What . . . is this?'

'Why, it's a record of all the Tamayo Specials that ended up in your belly. Sold to you on credit.'

'On . . . credit?' Miyuki flicked carefully through the notebook. 'Not quite sure I follow . . .'

'Mothers don't miss much when it comes to their kids, you know. Yours was on to you right from the start. Not too surprising, either. I mean, just think about how oily your pockets must have been – not to mention the smell. It wasn't like you could have made the croquettes yourself, and if they were a present you'd have no reason to shove them in your pocket like that. There was only one croquette stall in the neighbourhood, and that was Mrs Morita's. So your mother dropped by one day. Asked if by any chance her daughter had been stealing croquettes.'

Lost for words, Miyuki simply stared down at the notebook.

'Turns out you hadn't committed the perfect crime after all. In fact, Mrs Morita knew all about it too.'

Miyuki was speechless.

'She told your mother she knew you weren't doing it out of spite – that you were hungry, was all. She had no intention of scolding you for it. And before you ask, I didn't just imagine all this. Mr Matsuki happened to be there when the conversation took place, and remembers it well. He's the one who gave me this notebook, too. Said it turned up while he was sorting through the old lady's things.'

'So they all . . . knew,' murmured Miyuki, digging her nails into the back of her hand. 'I was such a little . . . idiot.'

'Actually, you were just a kid. Doing what kids do. Thinking they've got away with something, when in reality the adults are on to them from the start.'

'Sounds about right,' replied Miyuki, a mournful look in her eyes.

'Later that day, your mother went back around there to pay. With two Tamayo Specials you were running up a bill of fifty yen a day. Your mother made sure to drop by once a week and pay off your debt. That's what this ledger shows.'

'She . . . really did that?'

'She didn't want her daughter to be a thief. Any mother would probably have felt the same. At the same time, she worried that her own guilt about not being a better provider was making her go too easy on you – a concern that turned out to be justified when you became a serial shoplifter. She knew simply paying Mrs Morita off might not be the wisest choice. But after thinking it over long and hard, that's what she chose to do.' Nagare stopped and smiled. 'Of course, all this is just conjecture on my part.'

'But what does this bit mean? *To be reimbursed at a later date.*'

'Mrs Morita was a pretty stubborn lady too, it seems. She insisted it might just be a misunderstanding, and that she'd only be borrowing the money from your mother until you yourself came back to pay for them. That's why she kept such detailed records, see. Mrs Morita was waiting all that time for you to reimburse her.'

Miyuki sighed and wiped the corner of her eye with a little finger.

'If only I'd found her sooner. It's too late now, isn't it?'

Nagare looked her in the eyes. 'I'd say the important thing is that you've acknowledged that what you did was wrong, and it's never too late for that. The fact that you're here, showing contrition like this – the way I see it, that's what counts.'

'I'd like to hope that's true . . .' murmured Miyuki weakly.

'You live in Tokyo these days, don't you?'

'Yes. In Akabane, way north of the centre. Why?'

'Perhaps you could return this to Mr Matsuki for me.' He held out the notebook.

'But Dad,' cut in Koishi, 'didn't he say you could keep—'

'From Akabane it'll be a breeze,' continued Nagare, pressing the notebook into Miyuki's hands. 'Straight shot on the Ueno–Tokyo line, isn't it? Trains make life so easy these days.'

'Got it. I'll make sure it gets back to him.' Miyuki clutched the notebook to her chest.

'Oh,' said Koishi, who had finally caught Nagare's drift. 'I know – you can drop by Daishi temple while you're there. These amulets work a treat, I'm telling you.' She showed Miyuki the charm in question. 'I had a stroke of good luck just the other day. Bet they work with literary prizes, too.'

'Don't say that,' said Nagare, scowling at Koishi. 'If she wins, it'll be on her own merit.'

'Well, thank you both for everything.' Miyuki produced her silver-sequined purse. 'Can I settle up?'

'We leave the exact amount up to the customer,' explained

Koishi, handing her a slip of paper with their details. 'Just transfer whatever feels right.'

'I'll do it as soon as I get home.' Miyuki slipped her purse into her bag, then pulled on her coat and made her way out of the restaurant.

Mrrrow.

A tabby cat came padding over and nuzzled her leg.

'What a charmer!' She squatted and began massaging the animal's neck. 'Is he yours?'

'Drowsy, we call him,' explained Koishi, crouching at her side. 'And yes, he's ours. In a manner of speaking.' She shot Nagare a look.

He frowned back. 'Can't have an animal running around my restaurant, can I?'

'Poor thing.' Miyuki gave the cat a good rub on the chin, then got back to her feet.

Koishi scooped Drowsy into her arms. 'You like cats, then?'

'Oh, yes.' She rubbed the animal's cheeks. 'Tabbies especially.'

'You know,' interrupted Nagare, 'there was one just like him hanging around that apartment block. Where your old house used to be, I mean.'

'Really? Maybe I'll have to drop by and say hello.'

'Here,' replied Nagare, handing her a photo. 'The

woman holding it works as the building's caretaker. Said she'd been living around there for a very long time.'

'Oh,' said Miyuki, her eyes widening as she gazed at the photo. 'That, erm, does look a *lot* like Drowsy . . .'

'Keep it, if you like,' said Nagare, gazing kindly at her.

Miyuki took the photo, then dabbed at her eyes with her handkerchief.

As she began walking west down Shomen-dori, Koishi called after her.

'Take care, okay?'

Miyuki stopped, turned and bowed deeply.

'Koishi . . .' murmured Nagare when they were back inside. He'd folded his arms and was glaring at her.

'What? It's rude to stare, Dad.'

'What was all that about a "stroke of good luck"? I thought you told your father these things.'

Koishi chuckled. 'Oh, that? I only said it to encourage her. Don't worry, Dad. Nothing to report on *that* front.'

'Oh. Right. Well, if there are any . . . developments, you tell me. Got to report back to your mother, see.' He kneeled in front of the altar and lit a stick of incense. 'Hear that, Kikuko? False alarm. Looks like I'm not off the hook just yet . . .'

'Yeah, Mum, don't worry. Dad's in safe hands. I'm not going anywhere.'

Koishi set her amulet down on the shrine. Then she pressed her palms together, took a deep breath – and closed her eyes.

THE KAMOGAWA FOOD DETECTIVES

What's the one dish you'd do anything to taste just one more time?

Down a quiet backstreet in Kyoto exists a very special restaurant. Run by Koishi Kamogawa and her father, Nagare, the Kamogawa Diner treats its customers to wonderfully extravagant meals. But that's not the main reason to stop by . . .

The father–daughter duo have started advertising their services as 'food detectives'. Through ingenious investigations, they are capable of recreating dishes from their customers' pasts – dishes that may well hold the keys to unlocking forgotten memories and future happiness.

From the widower looking for a specific noodle dish that his wife used to cook to a first love's beef stew, the restaurant of lost recipes provides a link to the past – and a way to a more contented future.

OUT NOW!

THE RESTAURANT OF LOST RECIPES

Tucked away down a Kyoto backstreet lies the extraordinary Kamogawa Diner. Running this unique establishment are a father–daughter duo who serve more than just mouth-watering feasts.

The pair have reinvented themselves as 'food detectives', offering a service that goes beyond traditional dining. Through their culinary sleuthing, they reconstruct beloved dishes from the memories of their customers, creating a connection to cherished moments from the past.

Among those who seek an appointment is a one-hit wonder pop star, finally ready to leave Tokyo and give up on her singing career, who wants to try the tempura that she once ate to celebrate her only successful record. Another diner is a budding Olympic swimmer, who desires the bento lunch box that his estranged father used to make him.

The Kamogawa Diner doesn't just serve meals – it revives lost recipes and rekindles forgotten memories. It's a doorway to the past through the miracle of delicious food.

OUT NOW!